After a long dry spell, how does a single person find sexual satisfaction?

Davina's not looking for forever, just for tonight, but finding the perfect squeeze without using a professional is a turnoff. After all, no woman in her position could afford the risk to her image. The lonely-hearts listings in the paper trigger an idea—sign up to yoga and find a like-minded and available male to meet her needs.

Micah's dry spell doesn't just affect his sex-life, but the passion in his paintings. He's tired of the friends with benefits agreement he has with the agent and wants more—but without strings. A chance opportunity to enrol at Knights Meditation Haven and participate in yoga classes could be the answer to his problem.

Davina captures his attention, and she can't help the pull toward Micah either. By agreement, they both decide to explore sensuality together, along with the practice of Tantra. Davina's history, though, becomes a major stumbling block to the growth of any emotional attachment.

Can they discover a sensual world, one that surprises with the depth of emotion attachment and love? Only time will tell.

Please note:

The UK and USA share the English language, but there are many words that are spelled differently. Some words have extra letters in the British spelling, such as the word cancelled. In American English, it is spelled canceled. There are also words that interchange the letters c or s and sometimes z. For example, in America, you spell offense and in Britain, it is written as offence.

Examples of words you'll see in the book include: kerb, litre, centre, manoeuver, travelling and colour.

These spellings are **not** incorrect.

This book is written in UK English to reflect my Australian/English background.

WELCOME TO TANTRA

Dan Brennan M.D. describes tantra as, "an ancient Indian practice that dates back more than 5,000 years." In Sanskrit, the word *tantra* means *woven together*.

Many who have experience of the Kama Sutra as authored by Vātsyāyana, an ancient Indian philosopher, have likely heard of this practice, which uses sensuality and sexuality to reach a form of enlightenment. Many practitioners are introduced to this practice via meditation. (Please note, I am using **very broad terms** to describe the background for those with little to no understanding of tantra.)

Tantra also uses its own language, which you will see described throughout this book. Some of the terms you'll see, appear odd and are likely unknown. Below I'm listing some of the names and descriptions of what these parts or practices are.

Lingam: the phallus (penis)
Yoni: the vulva
Yab-Yum: Yab-Yum is a position where both partners are equally upright, the woman sat in the mans lap, her legs wrapped around his waist.

Note: There is a whole language associated, but these are terms I may use throughout the story of Davina and Micah.

Tantra is more than just sex, however. Should you want to know more, it is suggested that you take a look at any range of books dealing with this broad subject. Some titles to begin with include:

- *Introduction to Tantra: The Transformation of Desire by Thubten Yeshe*
- *Tantra: Introduction Guide Tantra, Philosophy and Traditions by Avaya Alorveda*
- *Urban Tantra: Sacred Sex for the Twenty-First Century by Barbara Carrellas*

You may even wish to look at Pillow Books (sacred texts often gifted to couples upon marriage, as a form of sexual primer) for some basic practices. The original Pillow Book is so called because the author tells about the Empress receiving a "bundle of notebooks" that she didn't know what to do with, and Sei Shonagon asked if she might then make a pillow of them.

Imogene Nix
Kingaroy, Qld
2022

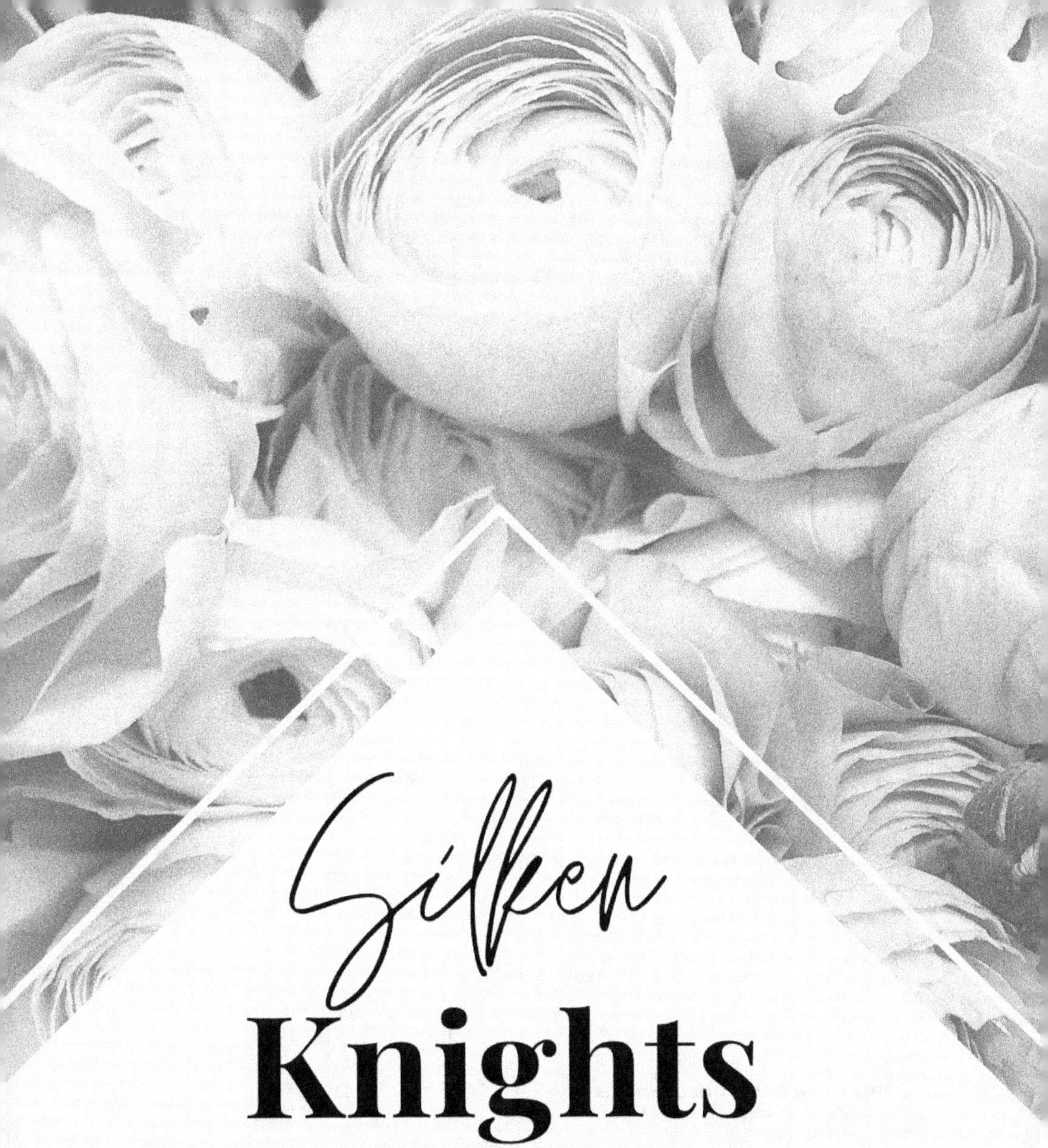

Silken Knights

Imogene Nix

CHAPTER

ONE

The clatter of Davina's bag hitting the floor of the restaurant had every head turning. She ducked, trying to avoid the scrutiny of dozens of eyes as she lowered herself into the seat.

The burn of gazes left her skin tight, heated with a searing blush. It took every ounce of willpower not to raise her hand and check, because she was sure it radiated from her skin. Instead, she let the silky curtain of her blue-black hair swing down, granting her some form of anonymity.

Her fingers wrapped around the arms of her chair, scraping it on the tile floor while sliding forward. Davina winced, wishing she'd been more careful. More like her elegant friend on the opposite side of the table. Especially since she knew which subject Elyse would investigate first.

"Made it, huh? How was last night?" Davina cringed at the interest in Elyse's voice.

There it was. Last night's abortive date. "Awful. I don't want to talk about it." Davina's muttered words barely travelled the length of the wooden table.

Elyse leaned forward, a harsh taskmaster for all her carefully up-swept blonde hair and piercing sapphire eyes. She craned and narrowed her gaze in the way she had since they'd been besties at school. "But he was *hawt!*"

"He also loved talking about himself more than he was interested in—" Her fingers twisted in the napkin she tugged from the table... On a deep breath, she stilled them, then exhaled.

Elyse rolled her eyes, stopping Davina's careful release of pressure. "You'll never get lucky if you don't drop your expectations, Dav. I mean, you're not auditioning prospective husbands. You were checking him out to see if he was worth the roll you need."

The single dirty fact was that she was looking to get laid, but her inner goddess refused to let her accept just anyone. No matter that she was only looking to burn off the sexual tension that welled in her belly every day.

"I'm not sure any of the men I've met could be the ones I want to get into a horizontal hoochie with Elyse. I want romance and—"

"Davina," the tone dripped with suppressed sarcasm, "you said it yourself. You've got a job, responsibility. At no point did you say you desired a guy who needs the regular seven o'clock booty call. You want sex without strings. The bang without the clang."

The stare of the woman seated directly behind Elyse had Davina's face flaming once again. Heat scorched her cheeks, and it took every ounce of willpower for Davina to ignore the accusatory stare.

"I..."

"Come on. You need to get laid, and we've tried just about every source of a respectable male who meets your requirements in this town. We've tried the online match making sites. You've tried the shopping centre and friends of friends. There's not much left. Unless you want to rent a body for the night?" A sparkle filled Elyse's gaze.

Oh God, no! Elyse was right, of course. Well, except for renting a guy for sex. She shook her head, but the seed of an idea flared as she remembered something she'd read on multiple dating profiles.

She was embarrassed to raise the idea and sighed.

"Dav?"

Davina squirmed in her seat, gaze sliding away from Elyse toward the entrance of the restaurant.

"We should order."

"Stop prevaricating, girl. Tell me what you're thinking, because I know that look." Her hand shot across the table and grabbed Davina's in a tight manacle.

"Look, I noted a lot of the guys on the dating sites said they *meditated.*"

Elyse's mouth curved upward, her blue eyes twinkling. Thoughts fled as Davina watched the flare of her gaze grow deeper. "Meditating?"

Davina swallowed the ball that suddenly formed in her throat and nodded. "Yeah."

"Let me think about it."

As if by magic, the waiter appeared at Elyse's shoulder. "Are you ready to order?"

❧

Micah McKay turned with slow and measured movements. In this space, he was in charge, of himself, his destiny and his vision. His pieces covered every shelf, as did prepared sheets of watercolour paper, silk paper, and even canvas. Light filtered down above him as he surveyed his kingdom.

Completed works sat on easels and others, framed and completed, fought for space in corners, stacked in preparation for the next gallery showing. The usual sense of completion and satisfaction he gained when surveying his work area failed to rise. A wholly unwelcome and unsatisfying emotion. Micah snorted at his inner ruminations.

The small ball of mirth melted while his belly tightened with agitation. "Face the truth, Mic, your work simply isn't enough to kill whatever you're missing." That had to change, because nothing could interfere with his work.

Clenching his teeth, Micah stalked to the piece he'd been hoping to complete—a room, redolent with shades of blue and peach, furniture draped with satiny fabrics... Right now, it resembled slashes of grey. His gaze moved to his initial sketches based on the photo he taped to the wall beyond. "What a waste." The pressure inside his brain swelled, turning his thoughts to mush.

Containing the frustration that grew and blossomed in his chest, he reached out, hand folding around the canvas, and yanked it from the easel. "I can do better than this!" His growl echoed, and he sighed, well-aware he sounded like a petulant child.

Karen had scurried from the room not five minutes ago, and he could still detect the angry tattoo of her heels at the far end of the house where she stomped to the kitchen.

His mind conjured an image of long red hair, tossing wildly against the hard slash of her jaw. The glint of fury in her eyes.

She hadn't coped well with his announcement that the casual sexual arrangement between them no longer met his needs. "I tried to do the right thing by both of us." His words floated into the atmosphere.

He remembered the way she'd flung her fury at him verbally. Words like careless, egotistical, and vile had tumbled over his head, and failed to do more than irritate him.

For the last four years, she'd been his agent and at some point, they'd moved to a friend's-with-benefits arrangement. He'd never promised her more than the relief she'd gained from an array of orgasms. He owed her honesty, but it wasn't like she was his *wife*. Her rage left him bamboozled. They'd both agreed at the outset of the relationship that if it was no longer meeting their needs, they would end their sexual association. That's exactly what he'd done.

He wanted more. A new challenge, a different way to fulfill his own needs. The sex had been hot, but his interest in her waned, burned away over the years, until all that remained was a casual connection and a semi-professional agreement.

"I'm not looking for a life partner and relationship. I don't have time or energy for that." His art usually filled him with a sense of completion. It was the source of his passion. Yet, right here and now, it couldn't fill the strange void in his soul.

His fingers itched to reach for... *something*. Usually, he would categorically say it was the tiny chalks, but not today. Which was the same as yesterday and the day before that.

"This is untenable." His voice filled with the unease that had wracked him for weeks.

His frown grew, and he felt the creases of his forehead deepen.

He'd have to go out and make his peace with Karen before she left. She was at least owed that courtesy.

D avina scoured the online groups listed locally on the social media site. There was more than she'd expected in the dearth of advertising mixed meditation classes, and she had the added challenge laid down by Elyse, which continued to ring in her ears.

"Go join a group, for heaven's sake. If they're mixed groups, you'll meet a guy. If those profiles are true, there's a plethora of single hungry males looking for a woman like you."

Oh yes, she thought. She really needed a man...sometimes. Her battery-operated-boyfriend— Bob—was buzzing slower in the last few months and in serious need of replacement. Sadly, though, the latex-covered vibrator couldn't wind its arms around her after a rotten day of representing soon-to-be divorcees!

Picking at the nuked meal, she bit her lip and scrolled through the pages of listings.

"Find Inner Healing at Meditators R'Us," she read aloud and flinched at the thoughts that rocketed through her mind. Visions of long aisles of people in similar poses and impersonal instructions had her stomach contracting. "Uh, no." No way could she go into a large group like that to seek a guy for 'personal growth!'

"Navigate your Personal Growth with Meditation, not Mediation." Noodles dripped as she snorted. "Nope, I don't think so."

Pushing the tablet to the far side of the breakfast bar, she sighed... Her phone burped and even knowing who it would be; Davina reached out, tugged it before her, and groaned. Pressing the answer button, she waited.

"So? Have you found a group yet?" *Elyse.*

Davina stabbed the plate, the sound shattering her composure further as she rolled her eyes. "No, I haven't Elyse. I'm reading through the listings and they're woeful."

"Woeful describes your sex life, Dav. You find one today, or I'm going to choose one and sign you up." She would, because Elyse was one of those take-charge kind of woman, where life was a challenge to be shaken by the hair roots.

"I'm looking," she groused. Not that she wasn't committed to finding someone, just this process seemed so cold and unnecessary.

"Well, I'm heading out on a date with Doctor Delicious, but I will check in on you and will be looking for a message once you sign up, girl. Nothing less than decisive action. Today, my friend." Elyse sighed, the echo on the line unmistakable. "Look, if you really don't want to do this, I understand, but nothing else has worked, and you said it yourself..."

Davina rubbed at her aching brow while surveying the efficiency of her kitchen. It was as empty as her life. "I know, Lys, but I can't look for a guy when every day all I see is the reality that marriage doesn't last." She'd known that since her earliest days, when her father had left their house and her mother had promptly installed another guy in her bed within a week. The carousel revolved so often, Davina had taken to calling the new men in her mother's life Alfie one, Alfie two and so on. Her father? He'd taken the hint, hit the road, and never looked back.

Marriage was nothing more than a reason to throw a massive party, according to her mother.

She should know she'd been married at least three, or was it four times? Currently, Maeve was on the upside again.

"Dav, you can't let your work dictate your life."

The little snort that erupted almost sounded like a laugh. "True, but it's hard to be enthusiastic when I see how relationships go wrong every day. Now go enjoy your date, Elyse, while I keep looking, and I'll let you know when I settle on one. I said I would and when have I ever not kept my promise?"

When Elyse hung up, Davina looked down at her phone. "Life would be so much easier if I were a lesbian, then we could hook up with each other." For a moment she contemplated the thought, then snorted, they both liked men and the sexual connection that came with them far too much. The bright side of that, though, was she'd always been able to count on Elyse to always be there.

CHAPTER

TWO

Micah looked up at the bland exterior of the building. It might be called 'Knights Meditation Haven', but there was nothing even remotely sanctuary-like about the cinder block frontage, the heavy glass and metal doors or the half-filled carpark. No, it reminded him of a bland office building without a soul. He almost turned around. Instead, he squared his shoulders because he'd been assured women loved men who meditated.

"Way to go," he told himself as he clambered out of his vehicle and glancing around. The meditation for beginner's session was full, Karly Knights had informed him, and he'd been lucky to squeeze into the last spot. Right now, though, it looked pretty darned empty. Perhaps they were already inside?

Musing as he wandered to the door, he considered this option. His friend James, a doctor from the local surgery, had insisted that this was the way to meet his perfect bang-bunny. He should know, having tried it out already apparently, not that it lasted according to James, but it was good for a short-term wham-bam option.

"I hope he's right."

Meditation. The word had him cringing. Thoughts of lotus positions and chanting really didn't appeal, but his work continued to suffer, and something had to change. Quickly.

The crunch of gravel broke through his thoughts, he turned, watching a small compact vehicle turn into the drive. It stopped beside his car, making it look like a hulking behemoth.

The woman inside the car got out, exhibiting the same amount of enthusiasm as he previously showed, and he watched, fascinated, as she swung her large tote bag over her shoulder with quick and efficient moves. Her midnight-coloured hair gathered at the top of her head glinted from the overhead shining street lamps.

Deep in his gut something lurched, and he blinked, spellbound, before she turned and closed her door, breaking his concentration. Twin lights flashed on the side of her car as she touched the tiny locking device in her hand and made her way in his direction.

Was she also attending the introductory class? He hoped so, because this was the kind of woman he wanted to meet. Beautiful, almost classically perfect until he caught the sight of her too wide lips, the tiny bump on her nose and the pencil thin brows. Her loose yoga pants and fitted exercise shirt screamed modern woman with an agenda, and the thought ricocheted that maybe she wasn't quite what he was looking for.

Ah well, hopefully there'd be other women there who would meet his criteria for artistic perfection. Something he appreciated daily. Yet there was something indefinable about her. It could be the confident way she strode toward the door...

"Excuse me, are you going in?"

The modulation of her voice grabbed him by the throat and shook his sensibilities, as nothing else ever had.

"Uh, yes. I'm attending the Meditation for Beginner's class. You?"

Her eyes took on a startled, deer-in-the-headlights look. Her pupils dilated, and he watched, intrigued despite himself at the flaring of her nostrils.

"Uh sure. I mean, yes." A delightful crest of red slid over the skin of her cheekbones.

"Well then, let's go in together." He grabbed the door, opened it wide, and followed her inside the building.

Davina gulped, more than slightly aware of the tall and unbelievably handsome guy behind her. Somewhere near six feet, he wasn't muscle bound but had that kind of toned look about him.

His hair, not quite black but more than a dark brown—russet came to mind—worn short but not militaristic. She detected a hint of curl, and she felt sure it was soft and springy to the touch. His face was all planes and his cheeks looked like chiselled granite. Davina was almost ready to melt right there and then.

He was the man she'd hunted for on the matchmaking sites with no success and when she'd finally taken a slightly less well-trodden path, here he was. An Adonis in loose pants and flowing shirt, turning up to her meditation introductory class.

A delicious shiver wanted to quiver its way through her body and yet she controlled it, even though her entire nervous system had become hyper aware and sensitized.

"Thanks," was all she could manage as she entered the building and the scent of incense wafted, cool air sliding over her skin while music, something deep and eastern, played low.

Once the door shut, the light mellowed to only slightly brighter than dim.

At the desk along the far wall stood a woman talking softly to three women, who then turned as one and trotted past, each with a small smile on their lips.

"Welcome! I'm Karly Knight and you'd have to be Micah McKay and Davina Elliott. Here for the Meditation for Beginners session, right?"

Davina blinked at the friendly tones, then the words hit her. The two of them... was there no one else attending?

"I thought the session was fully booked?" His voice carried a sharpness that had her wincing.

"And so it is, Micah."

Davina couldn't help herself. Her head turned, looking into the man's face as Karly spoke with soft, mesmeric tones.

"For these introductory sessions, I like to keep focus and it's easiest when I have only two students. Allows me to individualise your experience, so to speak."

The jitter that began when she'd first spied him moved further down her body, near her most intimate zone, and it left her tingling uncomfortably.

"Come, Davina and Micah, let's move into the studio." She beckoned them to the door on the left of the entrance way and they followed, Davina clutching her bag nervously.

Once they'd stepped over the threshold, Karly closed the door, and the intimacy of the space came close to overwhelming. The room was darker than beyond, with sounds which swelled from every direction, and padded cushions of jewelled tones littered the floor. A sweet scent of jasmine and citrus filled the air, and she stopped, momentarily lost in her thoughts.

A tinkle of laughter echoed, and she gazed at Karly. "Exactly what you should feel my dear."

"I... Uh, what?"

"You feel like you've stepped into another place. Somewhere that allows you to expand your senses. Isn't that right, Davina?"

Aghast that the woman had read her so well, Davina had no choice but to nod.

"Good then. Take a seat and we can begin."

Davina stowed her bag and noted that the man, Micah, had moved to a teal-coloured cushion, then settled herself on the floor.

"Now, I know neither of you has studied any form of meditation before, and I always think it wise to begin at the beginning. So, I'd like you both to close your eyes. Simply be."

Even as she did, Davina felt silly, aware of the man sitting in the room with her.

"Listen to my voice. Simply be yourself and breathe. Breathe in and breathe out. Feel the expansion of your lungs, the way you inhale, then gently release it back into the atmosphere..."

By the end of the first half-hour session, Micah had breathed and listened more than enough. *This wasn't what I signed up for.* No, he wanted to learn more about the facets of sexual meditation. To experience some pleasure while he had time to investigate more deeply the women he may meet. The woman he'd spent the initial session with, Davina, certainly interested him. It wasn't the frailty he'd caught sight of in her eyes and tried so damned hard to hide. Neither was it that she was downright *comely*—an old-fashioned word, to be sure, but one he embraced. Now he laughed because the old-fashioned term had never fit so well. It was an indefinable air that swirled around her, hinting at a sexual maelstrom just beyond sight.

She certainly intrigued him.

Micah blinked as he half listened to Karly and her suggestion of homework.

"When you go home, relax tonight. Let yourself just be with no attempt to meditate. Don't fill your mind with television. Instead, turn on some music that feeds the soul and eat a healthy meal. Then tomorrow and for the rest of the week, take time for yourself in a nest you've created. Prepare a room with sounds and soft places. Simply breathe and concentrate on the centre of your being."

"Fine." Davina's tone was anxious, as if she too were—he cast about for the right word—unsure of Karly's teachings. Not that he disregarded them. Careful investigation had shown him she ran the tightest ship in town for this kind of thing. It was more. He couldn't see himself assuming a meditative state in his house, with Karen coming and going at will and endlessly complaining.

"Micah? Are you listening?"

He blinked and grinned at Karly, hoping that would assuage any frustration she might feel at his inattention.

"I'm very impressed with the progress you've both made, but time is short for the introductory lessons. Come back same day next week at six and we'll go over what we've done and explore further." Karly ushered—the speed of which left him breathless and smiling —she'd obviously had a lot of experience with this, as she propelled them through the door and into the entranceway. The foyer now filled with others, laughing and chatting, ready for their session.

Micah moved to the door and watched as Davina scurried out and hurried to her car. She tossed her bag in and slid into the seat, then glanced in his direction before he heard the ignition kick over.

In that moment, he decided Davina was the woman he wanted to pursue, at least for now. *Oh yes, I'll be back next week.* He wouldn't miss it for the world. Now all he needed to do was make sure she was on the same page as him and ready to progress his interest.

D avina pushed the sofa out of the way, biting her lip and knowing that Elyse would find this far too funny not to laugh at. "Except there is no way she's coming over!" The words lacked strength and Davina slumped to the floor, gazing at the mounded cushions in jewelled tones she picked out.

Her emotions warred, and she swung from nervous, excited to dejected and back again. She'd been okay until the woman asked if she was redecorating, because surely her partner would love the colours chosen.

The memory left Davina's face flaming. "Do women only redecorate when they have a new lover?" The words echoed and mocked, and she felt foolish. "Of course not." But the weakness of her response had angry tears threatening.

It's what her mother had done with every fresh man in her life. A fact Davina had tried for years to block.

"Damn you, mother!"

If only the situation was that simple.

She was thirty. A successful woman. A lawyer. But the fact of the matter was, she had an itch she needed to scratch with a man. She didn't trust them to hang around, though. Not for the long haul, so rather than put herself through that, she'd concluded years ago, that casual hook-ups were her best and only option.

"Protection is key." Shame the words didn't instil any kind of confidence in her. Hell, the last six months had been a hell of a drought.

"I can sit here and wallow or do something about that." Anger pushed her from the floor as she gazed around the room, assessing. "No. Not this one."

Her three-bed unit gave her the option of a spare room. Not that anyone used it. If she met with a man—and that had been a long time waiting—she chose a hotel. Her mother never came to stay, and truthfully, that suited Davina. The mid-sized room she'd converted to an office and the other room was her haven. The bedroom.

Realisation dawned. "I can't set this up in here." If she were honest with herself, not that she was embarrassed by what she hoped to achieve. No, it was more about the intimacy.

She'd wasted the last hour moving furniture for nothing. Maybe she'd be better dismantling the spare room. It was wasted space after all, and Elyse never went in there.

Davina opened the door and considered the sparse interior. A bed. Two bedside tables and not much else. "Perfect." She could dismantle the bed and store it.

With quick moves, she unplugged the pretty bedside lamps, judged them to be perfect for her needs, and propped them in the room's corner. The bed itself, a white metal affair, was ornately pretty but hers from home, as were the bedside tables. Something about them jarred, and she stared as realisation dawned. "It's not the 'me' I am anymore."

What to do with them? In that instant, she knew she didn't want them or the reminders of what they stood for.

As she turned and looked in the lounge room's direction, she realised she'd kept the second, third and even fourth-hand furniture she'd moved in with. Cast offs and bits she'd bought cheaply when she'd first moved out of home and she'd ignored that, because it just wasn't that important.

There was no cohesion or theme. Black and grey chairs scattered around a scarred wood coffee table, but nothing to soften or blend.

Ugly yet functional. Mismatched.

"Kind of like me." Tears burned but Davina didn't scrub them away, because for the first time, she accepted she'd *settled* in her life.

The raging torrent of hurt, anger, and despair gathered pace, crashing through her like a sea. She surrendered to it. Let it wash over her.

When the tears passed, exhaustion tugged. "I need to change me."

Whatever had allowed the pain of her past to finally erupt also pushed her forward. "I need to change, and the first step is what I see around me." Decision made, she tottered toward the coffee table and scooped up her phone. A quick scan showed a lighter day. Nothing that required her physical presence.

Pressing the autodial, she called her boss, who she knew would still be at work. "Hey David? I need the day off tomorrow, I've checked my schedule and I've no court appearances. I'm going to pop out and see to some urgent business in the morning, then work from home, okay?"

"Everything okay, Dav?" She heard the worry. She never took time off, and it concerned him.

"Yeah, I'll be good. I just have some personal things to sort. I'll be back in on Wednesday." Even as she pressed the button, disconnecting the call, she could sense how easy it would be to sink into the fear. "I won't do that. Tomorrow, I can start again."

§

Micah stepped away from his easel. Frustration grew in his chest, larger and larger until it would smother him, and he rubbed at the ache deep in his chest. This painting was a passable facsimile of his vision, but nothing more. It lacked the passion and depth he knew himself capable of.

The magical quality, the strokes and smoothing of chalk he'd made his own, eluded him.

Just as they had for the last several months. If he'd been an author, he might have called it writer's block, but for a painter, it was death.

The light was perfect. His studio, overlooking the ocean, boasted one hundred and eighty degrees of glass. A clear domed roof, something he'd added after purchasing the property, sparkled as sunlight filtered down. The image he'd taken crisp and clear.

In his hand, the chalk crumbled as his grasp became evermore desperate.

His stroke-work exquisite, yet the tones just missed the mark. Moves that had become second nature refused to cooperate.

"Why?"

Karen, his agent and on-again-off-again lover, had left the room, muttering unintelligible babble about frustration being Micah's problem, her heels clicking with a rapid tattoo of fury. "That of a woman scorned." For a mere second, the miasma that surrounded him melted away, his fingers gripping the chalk as he leaned in, yet that small move banished the chink of spark, leaving him once again bereft.

Against the wall, stacked in rows, were canvasses, wasted to his mind as he'd attempted repeatedly to complete the work promised to the gallery. Time was running short, and that knowledge ate at him, riding him like a demon upon some hideous evil equine.

He turned, dropping the chalk into its slot and gathering up the cloth he wiped his hands on.

In the last week, Karen tried many times to interest him in what they'd shared, but instead of passion all he'd felt was a mild distaste.

He stepped into the kitchen, taking in the aroma of food. Spices teased his olfactory senses, stopping him in his tracks. The sigh he released was that of a man hard done by. If he stepped into the lounge, he might find her there. Two glasses of wine on the table, nestled in the deep mound of cushions. She'd done this before, the last time he'd attempted to end their relationship.

"Mic? I need you!" Her words filtered through his brain.

He stopped at the threshold and took in the view.

Her bright red merry widow fit perfectly, arraying every curve, her hair a curtain of red silk. Yet he remained unmoved.

"Karen, I can't do this."

She gave a moue, red lips glistening. "Of course you can, lover." Karen spoke breathlessly, as if overcome with emotion. "Come over and I'll help you, just as I always do." Karen pushed up, aware of the way her breasts rose and moved, creamy satin skin in pale contrast to the scarlet silk she wore. Every move meant to heighten arousal, but it left him cold.

"Karen, please. We can still be friends, but it's done. I can't do this anymore. I respect you too much."

Her cheeks blazed. "You don't mean that. I've seen your work and you need—"

"I don't know quite what I need, Karen, only that while I like and admire you, the sexual nature of this relationship is over."

Her eyes narrowed. "You've got someone else. Haven't you? You've been unfaithful."

He sighed, reached over, and assisted her up.

"No Karen. I haven't been unfaithful. I haven't taken up with another woman. It's just..." Helplessness threaded through his brain and entire body. *How do I tell her I no longer desire her? Without stripping what is essentially her away and damaging her irreparably?*

"But, in the past..." Tears glittered at the end of her eyelashes, the green now depths of embarrassment and loss.

He gathered her close, careful to keep his touch gentle and calming. "I like you a lot. It's why I'm ending this. Before you and I make a hasty decision, we'll regret. We've been friends and lovers for years, but it's no longer enough for me. I respect you too much to use you and I respect me too much as well."

Releasing her, he stepped back. "We, as lovers, have run our path. There's nothing more there for me to give you." He watched her eyes, noting the flare of recognition. Sure, for the first time, she not only heard but also understood. Their sexual liaison couldn't continue.

Karen sniffled. "You're sure?"

He tucked an errant strand of hair behind her ear. "Very much so. Now, go dress and we'll have dinner and see if we can find a way forward with the gallery situation."

Karen frowned. "I organised a casserole, thinking it would last in the slow cooker until..." Her words died away, and he knew exactly what she'd been thinking.

When they'd finished their encounter, they'd sit down to a meal. It's what they'd usually done, and his chest ached. He should never have allowed this to pass.

She moved swiftly into the bedroom beyond, leaving him alone to contemplate for the first time the destructive nature of their association.

He'd hurt her, the way she'd blushed, then paled. The scurrying gait.

On a sigh, he turned away and headed back to the kitchen, reached into a cupboard and pulled out dishes. He gazed at the white porcelain she'd helped him choose, and for the first time, he felt... *dirty*.

Shoving the emotion aside, he opened a drawer and picked up forks and spoons. The serving spoon lay beside the slow cooker, and pots of pre-cooked rice waited in the microwave.

When Karen returned, she was pale. The makeup she'd donned scrubbed away.

"I should apologise, Micah. You told me it was over, but I—"

"No need to say anything, Karen."

Her head bobbed up and down. "I'll get the rice." He watched as she opened the door with a jerk, the oven gloves he hadn't seen her scoop up on her hands.

Micah slid the heat stone onto the table and picked up the pot. "Apricot Chicken?"

"Your favourite."

He gulped, feeling small and mean. She could always be counted on to remember the important things, his favourite foods and even his parent's birthdays and anniversary. "I..." He swallowed the lump that rose in his throat. "I don't want to lose your friendship, Karen. While I'll understand if you can't be my agent, I don't..."

She smiled at him, sad, lips trembling. "I wasn't sure you'd keep me after today." She waved her hand at the lounge as she slid into her chair.

"I'll always want your friendship."

CHAPTER
THREE

Davina slid into her car, the sense of empowerment that filled her for the last couple of days fizzled away, like the dying rays of the sun.

She bit her lip and wondered if that man—Micah—would also attend. Maybe he wouldn't and she was worrying needlessly. There'd been a raw sexuality about him that tugged at her, but her discomfort was on a whole different level. She dismissed it. "It's the odd week, silly."

Since she'd taken a day off at the beginning of the week, so much had turned upside down in her world. Her assistant, Tabs, had resigned. Having fallen pregnant with twins, the morning sickness and stresses from her relationship meant she'd finished early to concentrate on other aspects of her life. The recruitment side wasn't going so well. "And that's yet another story!" The car slid to a stop as the lights turned red.

Then three of her clients had decided the divorces they'd filed for were just a tad too hasty. Jenny Amos, mother of three and wife of an influential local public servant, claimed, "I need to give it another go. For the kids, you know."

Her mother had called to let her know she was marrying the love of her life on a beach in Bali. "No need to attend, dear. Just me and Peter and an intimate ceremony for two." The giggle had left Davina wanting to gag.

"Is that marriage number four or five?" She'd have to check and change the names again in her address book and maybe even the address this time, she guessed.

Topping it all off, her father had called in a tizzy just this afternoon. "Good news! Laura is pregnant and due in February!" Wife number three with kid number six on the way. Yippee! Not.

"No wonder I have no intentions of marrying. Because life sucks when it ends." Heaven knew, she'd seen the result lots of times between both her parents and in her practice of family law.

At least her home was coming together, she thought, the engine idling as she waited for a set of lights to turn green. When they did, she moved forward.

The lounge was completed with a new corner suite in shades of mushroom, a rattan and glass coffee table, matching the new dining suite.

The spare room now resembled a functional meditation room, the bed gone, and an Asian carved wood side table boasted the two antique brass and glass lights she'd kept hold of, but everything else was rich jewelled tones. Deep cushions filled the floor space and made for a welcoming relaxation spot. She'd even sprung for a decent sound system for the room and mood enhancing soy melts, so she could totally relax.

The walls of the unit now boasted artworks of rainforests and landscapes. Hell, she'd even sprung for a Micah McKay original, though it set her back more than she'd expected. The depths and tones of the pastel taking pride of place in the room where she practiced her relaxation routine.

She drove into the carpark at Knights Meditation Haven, having sloughed off the worst of her problems, and looked forward to the session ahead. The car belonging to Micah was there, a large black

SUV, and she parked next to it. Tendrils of unease unfurled deep in her belly, but she fought them back.

"He's here to learn to meditate just as I am." Of course, that wasn't the only reason she was here, but his overt masculinity was too much for her needs.

She'd seen a couple of pleasant and innocuous younger men in the group that followed and considered that maybe one of them would be more her speed. They were more likely to be tender lovers and looking for an odd outing, ending in a passionate conclusion. That had always been her experience and had worked until this point.

Reaching into the back of the car for her bag containing the mat, and water bottle Karly had suggested she bring, Davina took the moment to breathe deeply, hold it, then exhale. It allowed her to gain control of herself, so she'd appear calm and collected.

Sliding out of the car and heading for the door, she realised he was waiting, watching her. A gleam in his eyes and that predatory look set fire to a small curl of heat in her centre. It smouldered, fed a little by the smile on his lips. Funny, she hadn't noticed they were full, or the deep blue of his eyes.

"Right on time!" Karly called out as she opened the door and ushered them into the small room they'd used last time. "Let's get straight into it then, shall we?"

He followed her in, the heat of his breath fanning the nape of her neck in a highly erotic and intimate manner.

Things moved and melted deep inside her. Things she wasn't expecting, and she gulped.

"Everything alright, Davina?"

She nodded furiously at Karly's query and headed to the side of the room, preparing to lose her bag while fumbling for a coherent thought. This wasn't her. Not at all. She was in control. Calm. Collected.

❧

She wasn't anywhere near as in control of herself as she may have hoped, Micah thought, watching the curvy Davina as she slid her bag onto the small area set aside for bags and belongings. Desire coiled, building in the pit of his belly.

The shake of her hands and the half furious, half terrified glint in her eyes were a dead giveaway that she wasn't in any way prepared for what might come. A hint of curl escaped the tight knot she'd used to contain her hair, and he noted the long line of her neck. Swan-like, he mused.

"Micah?" Karly called, and he turned, then paused, taking a moment to clear his head before moving toward the deep cushions Karly indicated to.

"Tonight, I want to explore your experience this week. Davina, how did you get on?"

Davina had slid onto a mound of deep teal cushions and exhaled.

"I, um, went and set up a meditation room in my apartment. I wanted it to be somewhere I could close away. Like a sanctuary, I guess." Davina's eyes moved toward him, half hidden by long lashes, and he felt the impact like a blow to his solar-plexus.

"What did you use, Davina?"

"I... ummm, I bought deep cushions and relaxing landscapes for the wall. A long low table with some lamps and bought a music system and incense-y-kind of stuff."

"Very good." Now Karly turned her attention to him. "Micah?"

"I just used the bedroom. It's dark colours, reds and browns. Guy-stuff." He hadn't really considered the environment for the practice of meditation, besides which, he really wasn't worried about the meditation side so much as the woman he'd met for sexual encounters. Wasn't that what he'd invested time in this for?

"Well, if you're comfortable there, that's outstanding. Today, before you leave, I have some literature for you. Different meditative practices that may interest you. So, grab the packets I've arranged before you leave. Now, time to practice..."

The half hour passed swiftly and by the end, Micah felt looser than last time. In fact, loose enough to wait until Karly had ushered them through the door before calling to Davina. "Wait!"

Davina stilled in front of him, white-knuckled fingers clutching the straps of her bag as she turned slowly. "Uh, yeah?"

"Look, since we're doing the introductory course together, I thought you might like to grab a drink afterwards? There's a little bar next door, and I thought…" He waited, watching as her pupils dilated, breath deepened.

"Uhh. Well, okay."

Inside him, the predator, tightly leashed, roared its approval.

Davina couldn't help herself as her body quaked. Micah had asked her for a wine. She wasn't sure if that was something to celebrate or faint over. He was the sort of man she usually avoided and yet; she walked with him, hand just glancing against her waist into a bar.

They gravitated to a small table in a corner, with two seats and sat opposite each other as the attendant made their way over. "Chardonnay, please." There was a husky quality to her voice that she wished she could banish.

He ordered a merlot, and she couldn't help but blink. The depths of flavour in the wine seemed to mirror the qualities of the man sitting opposite. She almost laughed out loud at the whimsy of her thoughts.

"So, how are you finding the introductory lessons?" He reclined in the seat as if wholly at home, and her mouth turned dry.

"I'm finding it interesting. Not quite what I expected, I guess. Maybe I expected more, you know, interaction."

He smiled, lips thinning, and yet the glint in his eyes shone brighter. "Interesting. I found the intimacy to be quite intriguing."

The oxygen in her lungs fled as the hunger she'd banked for some time fled. Was he *propositioning* her?

Unsure and at-damned-sea, while every part of her seemed to clench, she grasped for how to respond. Her veneer of sophistication was hard won and appeared the best way to deal with what he offered. Davina inhaled deeply. She shuddered as her lungs constricted, and she coughed. Loud hacking sounds. Embarrassment fled before her need to breathe.

He was up, concern in his gaze. "Are you alright?" Hands reaching for her.

Oh God! She nodded wildly, face flaming while raising two hands to ward him off. The paroxysm under control, she whispered, "I'm fine."

A waiter appeared, a glass of water at the ready, and Davina gratefully accepted it and drank deeply, thankful for the interruption so she could regain her thoughts.

Micah returned to his seat opposite her, watchful.

"Sorry about that," she muttered, knowing that she'd made a mess of any act she might assume, and shrugged. Time to just be her, she guessed.

Micah's smile had lost the smoulder of before. "Just so long as you're feeling better now."

"Oh, yes. Look about—"

His gaze narrowed on Davina's mouth, and she felt the kick of heat. "It's not important."

Frustration wove around her, choking back the sudden sense of having lost something important.

"Umm, so what do you do, Micah?" Their glasses of wine arrived, and she accepted the white with a tiny sip, pleased suddenly to have something to occupy her hands.

"I'm a painter. Well, actually a pastellist."

Now it was her time to narrow her gaze, move in slightly. "Really? You're not M McKay are you?"

His lips moved as he reclined back into the chair. "Yes, why?"

"Oh damn! I just bought one of your landscapes for my meditation room, but it worked better in my lounge."

"Really? Which one?"

She rubbed her fingers over her brow. "View of the Night Rocks."

The tiny wrinkles at the edges of his eyes crinkled as he smiled. "I love Night Rocks, but that one was special. It was the first piece I completed after returning here from Sydney. I spent a night out there, camping, taking photos. It was moody. Atmospheric to use a common term."

"It was the colours that grabbed me. The dark blues and crystal stars, the flashes of white on the rocks and—"

"You're a writer?" His words stopped Davina in her tracks.

"What? Oh. No, I'm a lawyer. Specialise in Family Law. You know, divorces, custody cases and things like that."

He spluttered on his drink, and it was heartening to realise that he, too, was human. "Really?"

His voice carried surprise.

"Sure. I've been working in the area for years, particularly divorces. I try to avoid anywhere kids are involved, though, sometimes I don't get lucky."

"Why is that?"

She sipped again, wondering the best way to explain without giving away her own history. "I can't stand the way the kids get used or abandoned after relationships break down. Too many kids out there with trust issues because the adults can't get it together."

Silence stretched between them. Then he sighed, "Sounds like the voice of experience, to me."

Taking another gulp, Davina swallowed as much as she could, not quite draining the glass, then slid it to the wooden tabletop. "Look, this was interesting, but—"

"Davina, if I said I was interested in you, would you be surprised?"

His words stilled her, every aspect of mind freezing in an instant.

"Davina?"

"I think we've both made a mistake here tonight. I have to go. I've got work in the morning."

Her hand speared into the bag, dragged out her purse in the drawing silence as she slid a ten dollar note out and dropped it to the table. "I'll... I'll see you next week." Then she beat a hasty retreat.

CHAPTER

FOUR

Micah stared at the easel, shocked by what he'd just achieved in the last twelve hours of manic work. It wasn't so much that his mojo had returned, so much as he'd needed to purge the sight of the horror on her face.

Davina.

Something about her had captured his soul, and he had to exorcise the hunted look from his memory. Yet what he saw in front of him now was a passionate and sensual woman, eyes soft and dreamy, lips upturned.

He reached out, almost touching the chalk marks, then pulled back.

Just like the night he'd visited Night Rocks, he'd felt compelled, more of an out-of-body experience.

It was the first work he'd completed in well over a month that had that emotional depth he'd felt lacking. But this... This was everything. There was the emotion, the depth. He could almost touch her soft skin. Her eyes shone in the light, and her hair appeared to be silky-soft.

The radiant aura mesmerised him.

It was a work that was sensual and carried the promise of intimacy.

Mine.

His reaction was immediate. Strong.

Arousal coiled like a spring...

The door to his workroom squeaked, opened wide, and light from beyond almost blinded him. Micah turned as Karen entered the room, her heels clicking on the wood surface, the *tap tap tap* driving into his skull like nails. It broke the fragile communion he shared with the painting.

"There you are! I was just about to put the kettle on..." Karen's bright chatter stopped as her gaze zeroed in on his easel. He heard her indrawn breath. "That's amazing Micah! The gallery will be ecstatic! Now, tell me you aren't sleeping with her and—"

"What?" His whiplash word had Karen rearing back, and he banked the anger that suddenly rose.

It was irrational in its suddenness, and yet he'd not wanted to share this.

"I'm sorry Micah, but it's amazing." Her voice dipped to a whisper as flags of scarlet shone on her cheeks.

"I shouldn't have spoken to you like that. I'm sorry, but Karen, you aren't supposed to just barge in."

"You've asked me in the past to knock and I meant to, but I'd been calling you and had this feeling. Look, that piece is amazing, and I know they'd be glad to have something of this calibre to display and you could name your price."

His sigh echoed in the sudden silence. "No. This piece isn't going to the gallery."

She snickered. "Of course, it is. They'll love it. What a wonderful portrait. Such depth and passion. But it looks to me like you've already—"

"Stop, Karen. No. It's..." He fought for the words that would end her insistence, but none were forthcoming, so he simply shook his head. "We'll find another central piece. I'll go through my stock room." He stepped back, grabbed up the rag to wipe his hands, and turned. "Did you mention coffee?"

Karen frowned, looked from him to the easel and back again. "Yes. Of course. Come on."

He followed her out, trying to banish the feeling that he'd made a mistake somewhere in this conversation that would come back to haunt him.

CHAPTER

FIVE

Tuesday again, thought Davina. Meditation tonight. Week three of a five-week course, and her belly jiggled with anticipation at seeing Micah again.

She bit her lip as she steered the car into position in the carpark outside Knights Meditation Haven. No black SUV. In fact, her car was the only one here. For a moment, she allowed herself to experience a shock of surprise and regret. Maybe her actions last week had scared him off?

"Oh well, I better get my act into gear." Elyse was pushing harder for her to find a guy. The only thing was, in her mind, Davina already had a guy. . . . Micah.

She shoved the door open and grabbed her bag, pressed the car remote and trotted to the door, aware she was a couple of minutes late. She'd timed it on purpose, so she'd have the room to settle herself. "All for nothing," Davina muttered and hurried inside.

Karly appeared harried. "Good, now you're here, we can get started."

The woman shunted her into the room as the word *we* exploded in her brain.

Micah waited on the floor for her, his smile welcoming with a touch of devilry about the corners, and her oxygen supply fled as surely as mist on a summery morning.

Davina scurried to take her place beside Micah, as Karly assumed her favoured position, and she closed her eyes.

"Today, I want you to take a moment to find your inner peace. The one you've been focusing on for the last two weeks." Karly's words were soft and calming. Relaxing.

The room was still and quiet and Davina allowed herself to sink into the practice, just as she'd been doing at home.

A rustle sounded, but she focused tighter, until the touch of a hand against hers shocked her. "Feel the touch of each other's hands. Focus on the connection between you. Feel the arc of nature's heartbeat."

The moisture in her mouth fled as the electric feel of skin to skin flared. Like a bright light behind her closed eyes and her breath caught.

"Feel the softness, his palm to yours. The way we connect to each other, to the earth and the atmosphere. Let yourself sink into that awareness, so it becomes part of you. Become one with it."

Between her legs, an insistent and hungry throb grew. The need she'd experienced when she'd first met him, burning hotter and wilder within her body than before. Hot enough to engulf her in the sensual haze that was floating around them both.

Davina fought it off, trying to listen to Karly's instructions, but every action roused her further.

By the end of the session, Davina was about to crawl up the walls. Keeping her eyes low, she hurried to collect her bag and shot out the door.

"Davina?" The sound of his voice left her shaking as the passion inside her reached out, yearning for him.

She stilled, then turned slowly.

His gaze carried the same hunger. "Give me a lift home?" The husky timbre was too much for her to bear, but at a loss to know how to respond. She simply nodded.

He followed her in silence, climbing into the vehicle after her.

Reaching into her bag took a lot of effort. Her hands questing for, then finding the keys. She shoved them with shaking hands into the ignition point.

"Davina—"

"No." She cut him off. "Just tell me where you live Micah, and I hope to God you aren't married or in a relationship."

His laugh was shaky. "Neither." He gave his address, and they drove in silence, the night closing around them, building on the facade that they were the only two humans needing each other right now.

At his home, an ocean-side chateau, she slid out of the car, the beep of the locking sequence loud to her sensitized hearing.

"Come inside."

She knew exactly what he was asking, but the erotic hunger was impossible to ignore. Her nipples engorged and pushing against the white satin bra she'd donned just in case this should occur, and the rasp of her G-string a reminder that the horniness was skyrocketing.

"Yes."

He shoved the door open, then tugged her into his arms. "You know what this means?"

She nodded, watching the movement of his lips, needing them now against hers. The throb of her body insistent.

Her fingers released the keys at the door, and she reached, hands clutching at his shirt. "Take it off. Let me see you."

Micah wanted to tear the clothes off Davina. She'd driven him wild with every touch and exhalation she'd made during the lesson.

Take it slow. The reminder was difficult to follow, but he refused to scare her away. Instead, he cupped the back of her head, dipped down so their lips were mere millimetres apart. Electricity sparked between them, and he held himself away for as long as possible before closing the distance and sipping at her.

Her hands clutched at his shirt, tugging insistently, and he reached down, cuffing her wrists with gentle hands.

"We've got time and I want to enjoy this with you."

She whimpered as he pulled her further into the dark recesses of his house. "I want you, Davina. I want to touch you. To pleasure you. I want my lips on every inch of your skin until you writhe beneath me. Tell me you want that too?"

Micah lurched just far enough away to catch the wild glint in her eyes. "Yes." Her answer was low, infused with the passion that jumped and burned deep inside him.

"Good. Then follow me, beauty."

He led her to the bedroom, left her standing in the doorway for an instant, as he reached for and found the matches.

Sliding one out, his fingers fumbling, he struck it; the light illuminating enough for him to see the starkness of her features. He touched the dancing flame to one candle, then another. In the corner, a small kerosene lantern illuminated the dark wood and red velvet bed. Large and inlaid with provocative scenes, carved deeply into the wood.

He smiled as he reached up, fingers closing over the button at her throat. Slid the fastener through, then dropped to the next.

Unable to still himself, Micah reached out, slid the carved wood clip from her hair, so it dropped a satiny curtain around her features.

He threaded his fingers through it, pushed it away so it caressed the skin of his arms.

She sighed.

Micah reached out, stopping the hand about to release the last button on her shirt. "Wait, Davina. Let me?"

It was a query of last resort. Her last chance because heaven knew he wouldn't be able to stop himself once the bounty of her breasts, outlined beneath the soft cotton, were bared to his sight.

Her lips curved.

Davina moved her hand away, and he covered the tiny button, still warm from her touch.

His hand shook, but he pushed it out, then reached up to push away the shirt.

It slid from her shoulders, forgotten immediately as he inspected the skin he'd uncovered. "You're exquisite Davina. But tell me." He leaned in and caressed the nape with firm sure strokes as she shuddered, "are your nipples light, like peaches or dark like plums, I wonder. Let's find out."

He slid his hand slowly, deliberately, around the skin of her back and she mewled.

Finding the clip of her bra, he released the white satin cups until pale skin sagged.

He swore, the urgency of needing skin against skin clawing at him. "Let me get this off." He reached down and with a jerk, Micah tore his loose tunic top off, so he was bared from the waist up.

His body burning now, he tore the bra from her waistband, where it had caught, and kissed her. A savage mating of lips and tongues, which she met touch for touch and stroke for stroke. Her fingernails dug into the flesh of his shoulders, but he welcomed the sting. It told him he was not only alive, but half naked against a gorgeous woman who welcomed and returned his passion.

The hard tips of her breasts scored him, burned where flesh met flesh and his hands slid down her back, shudders wracking her form as it screamed the passion that thrummed through her system. His grip settled on her hips, held her still so that his erection nestled into the apex between her legs.

The emotion so raw and overwhelming that he had to shudder through first one, then another breath, each more intoxicating as the scent of their passion filled the air.

He glanced down, pleased to note her breasts, smashed against his chest, were tipped by cherry-coloured nipples and, unable to help himself, he caught her gaze. "I want to taste them."

Her stomach quivered, nipples grazing, and he hardened further with a groan.

Her acquiescence was given with a jerky nod and a strangled "yes."

Micah slid down her body, laving the inches of flesh he moved against until he was before her, almost worshipping her on his knees. Opening his mouth, he captures one taut peak, tonguing the tip as she cried out.

"*God!*"

He fumbled with the waistband of her yoga pants, sliding shaking fingers inside, then pulled. Her panties followed, the string of them capturing his gaze. "*Naughty.*" Then that too disappeared as her mound, covered with carefully groomed dark hair, caught his attention and he slid his mouth against her belly.

"I have to touch you, Davina. *Please?*" His hands clutched at her, waiting for her to agree.

"*Yesss...*"

He cupped her intimately, thumb moving over the dampness he found there. Her sex quivered beneath his touch, and he dipped the tip of his finger within. "So beautiful, Davina. A temple for me to discover and worship at."

Her groan strangled as he dipped in, tongue glancing over the wetness.

"I need more. Please?" Her whimpers joined the shaking of her knees, and he knew it would take so little to splinter her right now.

He didn't want her alone. Not this time.

Together.

It beat like a drum, demanding more.

Everything.

Now he rose, sliding his arm around her as he wrestled with the snap of his pants, every movement urgent and driven by the raging thunder of his need. The pop as they sprang free, loud, then forgotten as he shoved at his underwear, toeing off his shoes. Micah slid a shaking hand beneath her.

She whispered a shocked 'oh' as he lifted her and carried her to the bed.

"I want you, Davina. So much I'm shaking. Feel the way you affect me."

She did, hand curling around his aching erection, fingers sliding over the tip so that he bucked involuntarily at the feel of her movement, nerve endings shrieking.

"I want you too, Micah. Don't let me come alone. Not this time." The huskiness urged him forward as he reached for the draw beside the bed, then palmed a small foil packet.

"Protection," he whispered as he tore the pack, releasing the condom.

Rolling it down, he couldn't control the jerk of his hips and he hissed, eyes closing involuntarily.

"Let me." Her hand slid over his. The last bastion of control fled as he shoved her back, straddled her.

"I'm not sure how long this is going to last."

She giggled, "Long enough I hope to make both of us happy." Her lips closed over his as she wound her legs around him and impaled herself.

Heat, silken and damp, surrounded him, and he moved, the rhythm as old as life, demanding and driving.

Hunger rose.

Every slide feeding the conflagration.

They rushed forward through the maelstrom, undulating against each other, fingers gripping, musk enveloping until there was nothing except their cries.

The fever burned in his blood, cresting as he lost control over the passion he'd savagely restrained, until the orgasm blew him apart.

His body exhausted, lungs burning, he slumped over the woman who even now clutched at him, her chest heaving under their shared exertion.

"Are you alright?" He could barely whisper, and she gave a languorous caress.

"Oh yes, Micah. I'm feeling excellent."

A small roll, and Micah snuggled into the counterpane, then pulled her against him and closed his eyes. *Just a moment...*

***

Davina woke with a jerk.

Where am I?

Memory hit, crashing, and she couldn't help the small stretch. Muscles continued to quiver, but an exhausted smile lingered. "Well."

The sound of snores had her head turning.

This wasn't quite what she'd had in mind when she and Elyse had started the planning of her campaign, but the result was very... satisfying.

For a moment, Davina considered the idea of staying, seeing what his reaction would be, but that fled when he jostled beside her.

I've never stayed the night, and I don't intend to change that now. This wasn't about building a connection or relationship, just about scratching that damned itch.

With a tiny huff, Davina slid out of the bed, casting a last longing glance over her shoulder, then set to hunting for her bottoms and G-string, sliding them up over her body while looking for the bra. She couldn't see it, but her button up blouse lay by the door, so she scooped it and her shoes up, beating a hasty retreat toward where she thought the exit lay.

Just inside the heavy door lay her keys, she picked them up, slid into her shoes and tugged the shirt over her naked chest.

Like a thief in the night, she carefully opened the front door and made her escape, wondering how she'd handle the meditation class next week.

Devilry raised its head. *Maybe you'll get lucky again.* "Maybe I will," she murmured, racing for her car, pressing the remote.

Davina slid into the seat and shoved the key into the ignition. Gripping the wheel, she inhaled. He hadn't woken or followed her; no lights illuminated the house. For a moment, a sense of loneliness assailed, then she brushed it aside. "It's not about forever. It's about sex. That's all I want."

She started the car and headed for home.

CHAPTER
SIX

Micah woke, layers of unconsciousness sliding away like mist. When he opened his eyes, the bright sunshine burned, and he groaned, rolling over. His hand reached and met emptiness.

Memories of Davina flared, and he started upright.

Out of bed, he noted her clothes missing and slumped to the bed. She'd gone.

"Dammit!"

He'd had every intention of asking her to stay, and maybe spend some time with him, share a glass of wine or...

The sex had been explosive, and his gaze settled on the book he'd purchased after reading the leaflets Karly had given them about the differing forms of meditation. The Kundalini ones particularly had appealed to him, and he smiled.

"If that's what made last night stand out, then I'd better read more."

But right now, he wondered what to do. Energy was flowing. He felt strong and in control. All good, but even with that, he felt something was missing.

He shrugged and headed for the bathroom. A shower, maybe a coffee, and he would wander into his studio. Maybe that would energise him?

He promised himself a glass of wine later and some more reading time, but for right now the light was good, and the urge called.

§

Davina tapped away at the computer, avoiding looking at any of the literature Karly had given her. After all, she'd gone to meditation simply to find a guy. Mission accomplished... But over the last week, she'd taken to practicing each night, enjoying the serenity that filled her in contrast to her day-to-day life.

The phone rang, and she jumped. A glance at the identification viewer told her it was Elyse. She'd been dodging her since Tuesday, the woman was like a bloodhound. Davina was sure she'd worked out something went on.

On a heavy sigh, she answered, "Hey Elyse."

"You've been avoiding me. Why?"

Davina slumped in her seat. "I haven't. I've just been busy." To her hearing, she could tell there was a giveaway kind of whine.

"Don't tell me you did the guy from Meditation?" Elyse practically crowed, and Davina flinched.

"What? No... No! I just—"

"Davina Elliott. I've been your best friend for twenty-five years and I know all your tells. I'm heading over now, and I want to hear everything in detail."

The line disconnected, and Davina cradled her now aching forehead in her hands. *"Why me?"* Not that anyone would hear her. Instead, Davina scooped up the pamphlets, particularly the one with Kundalini emblazoned and the couple in a serious clinch. Because that would—not fan the fire, because wildfires just raged uncontrollably—but encourage Elyse to start another.

She hid it in the meditation room she'd set up in the cabinet's drawer under the meditation CDs she'd bought and shut the door firmly.

She turned into the lounge, knowing Elyse would want wine to chat over, and her eyes caught sight of the painting of Night Rocks. The turbulence there reflected the one currently raging inside her brain.

Elyse was her best friend, but while she'd never shied before talking about exploits, this time it was *different*.

By the time Elyse arrived, Davina had settled herself and her nerves, sitting nursing a glass of chilled chardonnay and thought over what she could and would say. No details, because she wasn't a kiss and run kind of girl, but some broad-brush statements.

Elyse sailed in, tossing her bag to the lounge. "My, you've been busy. If this is what meditation does for you, I'm signing up!" Her gaze settled on the painting, "That's a Micah McKay work. I met him at a show when I was dating Doctor Delicious. They'd apparently been friends for the longest time. Shame he's a doctor cause that impeded playtime, but anyway."

Stalking into the kitchen, Elyse helped herself to a glass and the red Davina had already opened, then wandered back into the lounge. "So, girlfriend, tell me all the details. Are guys who meditate better?"

Davina wanted to swat at the heat growing in her face and gave a small grimace. "It's not like that, Elyse. I mean, maybe I did and maybe I didn't but—"

"Don't tell me the Evil Ice Queen of Divorce Court Number One has a guy who might melt her icy chastity belt?"

She started, then stared at Elyse. "Evil Ice Queen of Divorce Court Number One? Where did that come from?"

Now it was Elyse's turn to stutter and stumble. "It's ahhh... The guys from..."

She turned away and Davina pressed her advantage. "'Lyse?"

"Look, while I dated Corbin from Hedges, Mavin & Trott, he told me that's what all the guys call you."

Davina leaned forward. "What else?" Fury roared for an instant inside her then fled.

"He said they think you're like in a frozen shell. Frigid enough to snap-freeze them then beat them with law and logic cause that's all you sleep with."

Davina took a deep, long draught of her wine, then choked. "You've got to be kidding me?" The strangled words made Elyse look even more apologetic.

"I think they're all kind of scared of you." Elyse's lips turned down, and misery pooled in her eyes. "Look, I didn't mean to tell you that, so don't mention it, okay? Corbin was nice, but he wasn't looking for what I am, so much as a way to get back at you for wiping his nose in legal process he can't match or beat. It's why we only went out a few times. He got chirpy and told me the entire story and I felt icky. I never saw him again."

The shock poured over Davina, the flaming heat of her cheeks freezing in horror, and she clamped both hands on her cheeks as she dropped back into the chair. "Frigid? Snap freeze?" Her belly churned with nausea. "I'm a topic of conversation as is my sex life."

Closing her eyes wasn't enough to blank out the reality that they thought so little of her.

"Davina, they don't know you like I do. They don't understand what drives you." Elyse touched her hand and for an instant she almost gave into the urge to pull away.

When she uncovered her face, Elyse was hovering, hands fluttering. "I'm sorry I said anything. I didn't mean to hurt you."

Davina gave a sniff. "It's okay. I prefer to know. At least that way I can hold my head high when I walk past them. And I will." The bubble of bravado, though, was pretty shallow, and she needed time to consider Elyse's words and the implications. "Look, I slept with the guy, but I'm not up to talking about it, okay? How about we watch some television, because I'm not sure I'm in the right head space to go through the files I brought home to work on."

"We could watch that new romance you were asking about. It's available now for streaming."

"Sure, yeah." Her heart wasn't in it, but she knew Elyse was desperate to cheer her up. They were closer than the average friends. Elyse's parents had separated at about the same time as Davina's and they'd stuck together during the bad times, understood sometimes you just didn't want to talk, just needed some companionship that required nothing except being there.

"Bottoms up, then!"

Micah sat in the vehicle, watching for Davina, drumming his fingers. He knew it was a greater than even chance that she wouldn't turn up to their fourth session, and if that happened, he'd need to ask Karly for details. The woman might be softly spoken, but he had a suspicion she had a steely backbone and would refuse her address or even a phone number. He'd have to find another way of tracking her down if that was the case, but how?

The sight of her small compact vehicle entering the carpark left him limp, as a trickle of hopefulness bloomed.

"She's here." Quelling his smile, Micah climbed from his car. "Davina?" He called to her, watching as her head rose, turned a little to the side. Funny, from here though he could see she was surprised he'd turned up.

He strode over. "You left."

Her composure cracked just a little, her eyes betraying an inner turmoil. "I uh... I don't like to stay afterwards." She spoke so softly, he had to lean in to hear her.

"Look, I'm sorry if I came on too strong."

Her smile warmed the chill that had settled in his chest. "It's okay. I just... I had to go home. Work the next morning and all."

An unfamiliar feeling rose inside him, and he wanted to reach for her hand as they walked in the door together. Yet he felt foolish and unsure. Normally, he'd be the one leading the way, but his innate sense of people told him she'd shy at that. Instead, he jammed his hands in his pocket and followed her to the door.

On the door sat a sign, 'Closed for family reasons. Please contact the office to reschedule.' "Huh, look at that."

She stilled, the fragile composure she held around her like a cloak unravelling a little more. "Oh... Umm..." He noted the way she bit her lip and couldn't help himself. He gathered her close, careful not to spook her.

"I'm guessing wine is out, but what about a coffee? I'll keep my distance if that's what you want."

Her hand shook as she reached up to reposition her bag on her shoulder. "I'm not..."

A sob broke free and fear built. *What the hell happened?*

"Davina?"

"I, uh, got a phone call today. About one of my clients. I'm having a few issues coping with it." She swiped at her eyes.

"Come on. Look, I'll take you home. Make coffee and we can talk, if you like. Nothing more than that. Nothing implied."

"My car..." She waved in its direction.

"I'll arrange for someone to pick it up. My agent, Karen, is a skilful driver, or even my brother, Noah. He lives near here. Come on."

He ushered her to his car, had her installed, and reached out for her keys. She dropped them into his hand and looked out the window. Unsure what else to do, he checked the road and headed for his brother's place a couple of streets away. At the door, he engaged the handbrake. "I'll only be a moment." He was out of the car and at the door before he could allow her to stop him. Three imperious knocks and his brother Noah answered. The baby of the family. He was a chauffeur and had a night off.

"Hey little brother. I need a favour. I need you to pick up a blue

Camry at Knight's Meditation Haven and take it to my friend's house." He quoted the address as his brother stared at him.

"What? Why? I have plans—"

"It's kind of a favour for a friend with an emergency. Please, Noah."

His brother, sandy-haired and five foot eight, glanced at the vehicle, gaze narrowing as he took in the woman, her head bowed, hand over her eyes. "For her, right?" His stance changed, losing the stiffness he'd shown before.

"Yeah. Please Noah."

"You owe me." Noah retreated inside and shut the door, leaving Micah standing there staring at the wood. With a shrug, he headed back to his car.

"Is everything okay?" Her voice carried breathlessness, and he noted the pink tinge to her eyes. She'd been crying and tried to hide it from him. It burned him to think that someone or something had made this occur to what he had already deduced was a fiercely strong woman.

"Yeah, Noah will drop your car over. He's a professional chauffeur so he'll drive it carefully."

She looked nonplussed. "Oh. Okay then. Look, thanks for this. I didn't realise how much this hit me until I got there and found the door shut." Her hands flew, fluttering like the movements of a fragile bird, and it made the protective instinct within him rise.

"Not to worry. Let's get you home and coffee. You clearly need a friend to talk to."

At the apartment block, he pulled into the visitor parking and waited as she unfastened her seat belt. "You're okay with me coming inside?"

She nodded. "Yes. I really want you to come with me."

Davina climbed out and he trailed her to the front door. With quick, efficient moves, he entered the unit, his eyes settling on the painting above the lounge. "Love the painting," he deadpanned, and she giggled, just a tiny sound, but it heartened him.

"I like it too. Look, take a seat and I'll put the kettle on." He watched as she moved into the small galley, the cut out allowing him to watch the way she flowed around, clearly at ease in her own environment.

"So, why me?"

She whirled; surprise etched across her face. "I really don't know. I could have called my friend Elyse, but you..." Davina squirmed.

"It's okay. I'm happy to listen, just I'm surprised you didn't call one of your friends."

The mug on the bench thudded, the sound reverberating. "I don't have a lot of friends. I've got, I guess you might call them issues."

"Ah." He understood that, as many of his peers were similar. Hell, he was aware there were others who'd say he did, too.

"One of my clients was attacked overnight by her partner. The restraining order we'd applied for was denied." Her back was turned in his direction, but he could clearly see the white of her knuckles.

"Is she alright?" He wanted to stand and make his way over to her, but the stiffness of her back warned him that wouldn't be so wise at this point.

"She will be, but she lost the baby. She was five months pregnant with a little girl."

Pain radiated in her voice, and he closed his eyes, unable to understand how anyone could do that. Hurt a woman and kill their child. "I'm so sorry, Davina." The words didn't come close to expressing his sympathy. It certainly didn't quell his rage at the unnamed excuse for a human being who'd caused such unimaginable harm.

"Yeah, me too. They got him, but it's too little and too late. He's sitting in a nice, cosy jail cell. She's in hospital tonight, broken because of that bastard, and I can't help but feel that if I'd done a better job, she'd be okay. Safe with the baby to look forward to."

She slumped, and he was up, moving in her direction. Grabbing her as she dissolved before his eyes. The jagged, wrenching tears overwhelming. He held her tight as she shook, her tears soaking through his shirt until the paroxysm stopped.

"I'm ahh... I'm so sorry." She squirmed. But he kept her close, amazed that this woman, strong and valiant, had trusted him enough to fall apart in his arms.

"It's okay, Davina. You need a friend, and that's me right now. Trust me, if you need me to stay I can." He meant it. There was no way in hell he had any intentions of leaving her alone to deal tonight.

"I tried to get the restraining order before, and they said..." she hiccupped, "that he didn't pose enough of a threat. *How can that be?*"

There was no answer that could even remotely fix the problem. "You did what you could. I'll bet you tried every avenue, didn't you?" The surety had him guiding her to the lounge. "I'll bet you even offered to go above and beyond."

"I told her she could stay with me." She sighed, "but she said no. She was going home and would not let him get away with standing over her. It didn't matter that he'd made verbal threats and claimed the baby wasn't his, that having the brat was undermining him." Davina shook her head. "I just... There are just days I hate my job."

"So why do you do it?" The question slipped out before he could call it back.

"Because my parents had such an acrimonious divorce. Neither has spoken to the other since then and I just... The kids are left with their lives smashed, no innocence left, and it's not right. I do it for them. For those left behind who have to get their lives back. It's not enough, but I do what I can."

His respect for her grew, and so did the emotional attachment.

Micah looped a strand of her hair over her ear. "Have you eaten?"

When Davina shook her head, he rose. "Well, I'm a decent cook so if you're game to let me loose in your kitchen, I can fix us something."

The frown she gave him furrowed her brow. "You don't have to do that. You've already been great listening to me whine and cry."

It took every ounce of his will to avoid the clenching of his jaw. "You're kidding right? You've had a rotten day and you deserve a little TLC. So, let me do that. Sit back and would you like a glass of wine?"

Her head cocked. "Actually, that would be fantastic."

"White, yes?" He remembered she'd ordered Chardonnay last time they'd had drinks together.

"You've got an excellent memory."

"Goes with the job, really." He moved into the kitchen, pleased to note it had most of the basic tools. A quick glance in her freezer told him she wasn't really a cook. There were frozen meals galore and only a couple of chicken legs, some steak and a packet of pork spareribs. At least there were frozen stir-fry vegetables. He hunted through the cupboard while defrosting the meat in the microwave, grabbed some rice and set about soaking it to prepare for cooking.

After a short while, she wandered in, perched herself on the counter. "A decent cook, huh?"

She watched his movements as he sliced and set up a quick and dirty marinade.

"My mother was an assistant cook at a school, never wanted the top job because she hated menu planning. Taught me and my brothers and sister everything we know." He threw the meat into the bowl and turned back to the stovetop.

"How many siblings do you have?"

"Two brothers, Noah and Simeon, and my sister Miriam."

Her eyes rounded. "They're very... biblical."

"Yeah," he chuckled. "My dad was a cleric, so it kinda went with the job. We grew up with the whole nine yards, church every week-end, usually several times each weekend. The youth groups but they weren't, you know, over the top and conversionist."

"Were?" Davina prodded.

"My dad died when I was twenty-seven. A heart attack in the middle of the sermon. Mum was in a car accident three years ago. Didn't pull through."

Her lips formed a small 'o.' "I'm sorry to hear that."

"Yeah, it was tough, but we're all pretty close. Still do family meals every Sunday, rotating around our houses. But what about you?" It made sense that the key to her self-imposed wall had something to do with her family. He wondered if she'd answer the question.

"My mum and dad broke up when I was five. Dad's on his third marriage and his sixth kid is due in a couple of months, while mum is getting married next week in Bali. Marriage number five there."

"Ouch. Tough that."

Her shrug was a little too pat, as if she'd practiced it for years. "You get used to it. At least mum didn't move me around. She would move them into the house because it was all too hard to pack, move, and arrange the change of mail more than anything else. The name change seemed to be about her level."

Rancour seeped from her words. His gaze narrowed, but he let the comment slide for now.

"Do you see them much?"

She shook her head. "They're pretty busy with their lives and I seem to remind them of what happened before. And I don't mean the good times."

"Oh." He thought over her words. "She didn't have any other—?"

"Oh, heaven's no! That would have strained her body too far, according to her. I was enough for inducing stretch marks and having to endure school meetings and so on. But it's okay, I have Elyse, my best friend. I've known her since about then, and her parents broke up at the same time. And I've got my work. It's fulfilling."

Just keep telling yourself that. Clearly, she wanted to believe it. Maybe had spent years reinforcing it. Micah wasn't buying it, though. "Look, what are you doing Sunday? Come join us for lunch. It's at my place and I can promise you a home cooked casserole."

"Oh no, I couldn't."

He turned back to the stove, slid the vegetables out, noting that they'd overcooked slightly and tossed in the meat, stirred the rice as he considered how it might be observed by his siblings.

"I'd really like you to." He meant it too. Not that he intended to inspect his feelings just now.

"I—"

"I'm not taking no for an answer, Davina."

SEVEN

"What do I wear to a Sunday dinner, Elyse? I mean, its family, just him and his brothers and sister, but do I dress up? Wear a skirt?" Holding the mobile in one hand, she held up a more formal skirt suit. "Or would you go with a dress? I mean..." she dropped to the bed and held her head in her hand. *What the hell am I doing?*

"Girlfriend, jeans and a nice blouse, a set of heels and some makeup. Unless... Is it a date?" Elyse's voice carried the question she desperately wanted to avoid because she couldn't answer it.

"I, uh, no." He'd given her instructions to arrive at eleven, not to bring anything and be prepared to have fun. That could mean anything.

"So, go comfortable. I mean, what's the worst that can happen? You can't be too worried about the ramifications unless you're sweet on him. Is that the case?"

"Oh, no!" The vehemence belied the truth. The seed of a relationship was forming, even though she really didn't want that to be the case. Relationships were scary beasts that could break you when it went wrong. She'd seen that more than once. Been around for the messy clean up, the tantrums and screaming matches. The recrimi-nations.

"Good. Then go have fun. Meet some new people, be fed by someone you told me who can cook and enjoy. Now, I have to get ready for my date."

That caught Davina's attention. "Date?"

"Doctor Delicious rang me up. Said he missed my sunny face and would I be available for a restaurant lunch. I, of course, accepted. He was seriously good in the sack!" Elyse fanned herself and even through the tiny viewer of her phone screen, Davina caught sight of the facial expression that expressed completion.

"Well, I hope it ends up as you hope it does then. But for now, I think I'm going to go middle of the road with a casual dress and heels. Thanks for your help, Elyse. I'd better get moving."

Ringing off, her gaze settled on a bronzed dress with tiny-sprigged flowers and a large cream coloured belt. *I've got just the right shoes to go with that.* Fishing around in her closet, Davina found the shoes, then hurried to the bathroom, showered in under ten minutes and shaved her legs, blow dried her hair and tied it up in an informal bun and applied the minimal makeup. Sliding the dress over her body and stepping into her shoes, she turned and inspected herself in the mirror.

No classical beauty. At least she was curvy in all the right places. Her eyes, shades of brown, were okay, and her dark hair shone. "Well, that's as good as it's going to get."

She grabbed her bag, phone and keys, then galloped from the unit. She didn't have time to muck around if she intended being on time.

At Micah's front door though, she stopped, took a deep steadying breath, smoothing the dress over her now jumping belly, and knocked.

The door opened. A statuesque beauty with sandy hair smiled. "Hi, you must be Davina. I'm Miriam and was told to meet you and bring you inside." The woman's grip was lethal as she tugged Davina inside. "Micah hasn't told us much about you, only that you're taking meditation classes together. Dad would have had a cow, but we're all individuals, you know. By the way, I'm a Doctor at Saint Frances' Hospital and I think you've met Noah. Simeon will be here shortly, he's got the service at the Church of Saint Helen to complete, which is a hoot because he was the least churchy of us as kids." The rattle of Micah's sister was settling, allowing her to slough off the nervousness.

"So, you're a doctor, Micah is an artist—"

"Pastellist. Better get that terminology right," giggled Miriam.

"Sorry, Pastellist, Noah is a chauffeur and Simeon is a priest?"

"Pastor. Thank God! Otherwise, no kids and he's got two already with his wife, Fenella."

The crowd would be larger than she imagined. "O-kay."

"Don't be too concerned. We're a pretty wild bunch, but friendly enough. Unless you're into paganism, then Simeon might have something interesting to say."

Micah stuck his head through a doorway. "Miriam, stop scaring the guest. Davina don't worry. Simeon is a peaceable guy and won't care what you believe so long as you're nice to Fenella and the kids. Welcome."

The short wave of Davina's arm felt ridiculous, but she didn't feel comfortable wandering over and kissing him, even though he looked eminently tasty. *Don't go there!* The caution was ignored, however, by her unruly body, as it heated.

"Uh hi, Micah." The word croaked out, and she wanted to groan at the give-away once she caught sight of Miriam's hastily controlled grin.

Micah winked as Miriam retreated and disappeared around a corner and he darted out, bussed her on the cheek before sliding away. "Glad you could make it. It's just a family dinner, but we try to do this every week. Keeps us all in touch, you know. Now, if you follow Miriam, there's wine, juice, soft drink and water laid out."

"You don't need help in the kitchen?"

His eyebrow raised. "I saw what's in your freezer. Unless you have mad hidden skills, you go take a break."

Davina snickered, "No, sadly. I can boil water and cook toast. That's about my limit."

When he smiled, her stomach melted like a pool of ice. "We'll have to do something about that then, won't we?"

Micah trotted back to the kitchen, leaving her standing there watching him retreat.

❧

His body ached by the end of the meal. Not from food, but from his hunger of a different sort.

Davina had joined the banter slowly, but his siblings clearly thought she was okay as they insisted that both he and Davina watch the sleeping children while they cleared up.

"They're great, your brothers and sister. Even Fenella."

He nodded slowly, understanding the Fenella comment, given she was pretty intense in the mothering department. "It's great that we're tight. I mean, we'd been like that before, but after Dad, then Mum... We kept up the routine and it feels right, you know?"

Cocking her head to one side, Davina stared at him. "I guess."

Of course! You're an idiot! "I mean for us..."

The silence stretched for a long second. "It's okay. I really don't know my brothers and sisters. We live different lives, but that's okay, right?" Davina's voice echoed with forced surety.

The thing was, he didn't think she believed her words any more than he did. "I didn't mean—"

"It's okay Micah. Every family is unique and mine is just... disjointed? Last time I saw Dad was about four, maybe five years ago, when he married Laura. He demanded I turn up to the ceremony and reception in the week before my bar exam. Before that, I hadn't spoken to him in ages."

"And that's why you... Never mind. Look, will you stay? Please?" He reached out for her hand.

"I don't know. I mean, I've got work tomorrow and I'm in court most of the day, so I need to make sure I'm ready, have my papers in order and—"

"Davina?"

"What?"

"*Please.* Not for anything just so we can talk or..." Actually, he didn't know why he'd asked her to stay. He wasn't thinking of the sex, just he wanted to spend time with her.

The panic on her face was met with, "I can't. Not today. In fact, I should go." She rose as the sound in the kitchen rose to a crescendo.

"Wait. Maybe—"

Wisps of hair escaped from her loose knot and fluttered as she shook her head. "Goodbye Micah." Davina was down the hall before he could call her back, so he trotted after her, throwing an absent "back in a moment," over his shoulder.

Already reaching for her keys, Micah put on a spurt of power. "Wait!"

Davina stilled, rigid enough that a gust of wind might shatter her.

"I spoke without thinking. I didn't mean to hurt you." He slid an arm around her waist. So their bodies touched.

"It's okay."

The thickness of her voice tore at his guts, flaying him from the inside. "It wasn't. It's just I have a close family and I don't understand... But I want to, Davina. Let me in."

Her strangled inhalation spurred him to turn her. Her face, now pale with silvery tracks, made him stop. *What? What is different this time? Why do I care?*

"Let me in Davina."

"I don't want a relationship, Micah. That's not what I came here for." Her bottom lip quivered, and her voice cracked.

"Maybe not, but both of us want more this time. I'm willing to try Davina, but are you?"

She backed away; eyes wide open. "*No.*" Fear punctuated her words as she trembled. "Because that only leads to hurt. Been there, done that. No more."

Movement's jerky. She shoved the key into the car door, ripped it open and climbed inside while he watched, tense and unsure what to do next.

As she started the car, he tugged on the door. "I'm not giving up. Not on you and not on us."

With that, he slammed it shut, hoping he'd planted a seed of doubt and stalked back while she jerked the car forward, out of the driveway and onto the road.

Tuesday morning passed in a blur for Davina. The day was eventful as usual, with a vitriolic attendance at court. Jane —her client—arrived on the arm of her brother. The bruises on her face testament to the ferocity of her soon-to-be ex-husband's attack. The judge refused bail for him, and she and Jane both breathed deeply as they left the court precinct, satisfied that until the next attendance, she'd be safe. "You're going home with your brother?"

The woman merely nodded, her face downcast, and Davina as she entered the offices. Her new assistant met her at the door. "I'm not so sure this job and I are meant for each other. I've had six clients complain about restraining orders being ignored, two refusing to pay because they lost out in child support and another—"

"*Woah!* Stop right there. Why are you taking calls about Child Support and...?"

"Mr. Livingston said I was to help him out while you're in court but—"

Anger and understanding bloomed. "I'll sort Jeffrey Livingston out. Your job is my aide and—"

"I've only just started, and already my inbox is overflowing. I don't think this is going to work. So, I'll stay until the end of the week, but I've already been offered a job with shorter hours and bigger pay. I start on Monday."

Davina stared at the pocket-sized redhead; her mouth open. "Umm. Well, if you feel like that, maybe this isn't the place for you. Grab your things and head on home. I'm sure a day and half 's pay is better than nothing."

Fury wound through her. *How dare they?* With enough work on her hands, the histrionics of a new hire and the machinations of a lazy associate were just a step too far.

The woman gaped. "But what about the rest of the week? I was going to use that money for a cruise and—"

"Then I'm sure as you reorganise your finances from your new high-paying job, you'll be able to find the money. Please clear your desk and I'll have someone grab your keys and delete any authorizations you may already have." Davina took great delight in stalking away from the woman.

At Jim's door, she hesitated, firmed her shoulders, and marched into the executive office. Melony, his assistant, sat at the desk. "Something wrong, Davina?"

"Lots, Mel. I need to speak to Jim, urgently."

Melony frowned, tapped at the computer. "He's free for about ten minutes, but after that, he's on the clock."

She reached for the door handle and turned it. Jim, her boss, had just turned sixty the week before. Slim and well groomed, glasses perched on his nose hide clear grey eyes which matched his suit.

"Davina. Something wrong?"

"Lots, Jim. Jeffrey Livingston grabbed my new assistant and made her take the calls from Child Support services and payments, and she only started yesterday and is overwhelmed enough with my work. That's not her job, and he's using this ploy to get out of his own work. Plus, she's just informed me she's accepted another job with 'fewer hours and more pay' starting on Monday. I told her that her services weren't required. I'm going to ask Melony to delete her from the system and get her keys, but—"

"Jeffrey is a tick." His heavy huff of breath shared his frustration. "One I need to deal with, so leave that with me. Melony will chase the authorisations and keys, but you need an assistant. You almost drowned in paperwork when your last one left." He stood, scratching his head, and turned to the window, looking out over the lane below. "You work too many hours as it is, Davina."

They'd had this argument in the past. It always ended up in a mad tangle, with no outcome. "I do what's needed to complete my job, Jim. But there's no place for people who aren't committed to the job. We do too much Legal Aid work to have slackers." She pointed in the general direction of Jeffrey's office.

He gave a weary nod and slumped into his seat. "I know. I've tried to avoid conflict, since most of us deal with it daily. But of course, you're right. I'll deal with Jeffrey today. That doesn't fix your assistant or lack thereof, though."

Davina gave a careful shrug. "I can manage until we get the right person. Just make it quick, okay? Now will you ask Melony, or should I?"

"You go, and I'll talk to her immediately." He shooed Davina from the office while lifting the phone to pass on instructions. As she moved by Melony's desk, the woman gave her a thumbs up and mouthed, 'sorting it now,' to her.

Leaving the executive offices, Davina palmed her phone and dialled Karly at the Meditation Haven to cancel her session. "Oh, that's fine. I'll let Micah know and we'll simply reschedule since I wasn't around last week, anyway."

Davina ground her teeth silently. *Not at all what I wanted.* No, truth be told, what she wanted was to miss the session and not have to deal with Micah, either. Going the Micah route led to quicksand. "And I've got enough of that already."

❧

Frowning at the phone, Micah embraced the frustration that gnawed. "She's dodging it."

"What?" called Karen from the front of the gallery.

"Dammit." He'd had no intentions of saying anything to the woman about Davina but knew that was a moot point the moment Karen stepped around the corner, her head cocked to one side.

"So, who? What?"

Trying to avoid Karen's questions was something he knew from their long association wouldn't achieve anything. Instead, he mentally girded himself. "Davina, the woman I've been..." *What best would describe the situation?* It wasn't a relationship as far as she was concerned and wouldn't be if he couldn't encourage a change of mind. His own inability to encapsulate it in one word was part of his problem with their status. He shook his head, trying to clear the fog that clouded his thinking. "The woman I've been seeing. We were supposed to be meeting tonight at meditation—"

Karen's eyes glittered with interest. "You've said nothing about a woman or meditation. Do tell." She leaned in closer, and he felt trapped.

"I'm uh... I met Davina at meditation. After we..." He rolled both hands and Karen nodded her understanding, then tapped her full lips with scarlet tipped nails.

"Yes, I get that we're over and I'm past my hissy fit. But you've kept this silent."

"For a reason."

Her grin couldn't zap his feelings of discomfort. *I don't want to talk to you about her.* But she stood there, waiting.

"Fine! She's lovely, and I'm hoping she thinks I'm special, too. Now can we get on hanging these bloody works?"

Heaven help me, let Karen take the hint and leave me alone! He turned back, creating a physical barrier, reinforcing that he didn't want to discuss it.

One moment, then another passed before he heard her mutter, "fine," and retreat. It was all Micah could do to restrain the urge to sigh. He didn't know how next to reach her. Instead, he vowed he'd give her a couple of days, then if he didn't hear, he'd contact her by phone, see if there wasn't some way he could connect on a more than physical level with her.

The door closed behind Davina with a whump that her head was sure sounded more like a slam. The horrendous week finally at an end, Melony assured her the replacement personal assistant was due to start on Monday. Jim had thrown the gauntlet down to Jeff that under no circumstances was he to palm off work to anyone else, and the tricky divorces she'd been overseeing for the last couple of months were concluded.

With Elyse on a date with her "hottie healthy" and a glass of wine riding high on Davina's agenda, she slumped into her seat.

The peal of the doorbell had her eyes closing momentarily, but the trill continued and, unable to ignore it, she rose and answered the imperious sound. "Micah!"

His eyes glinted in the doorstep's light, and she ushered him inside. "I was passing by and thought I'd drop in. Find out if you wanted to catch up for a wine some time tomorrow? I could pick you up?"

Her gut constricted as the fear she'd been trying to ignore rose again. "I... uh, I've got a lot happening right now, Micah."

"I see."

His tone told her he probably did, and she winced, aware that he knew she knew. "Look, I'm not sure any of this was a great idea and allowing either of us to continue with this will only make the end worse." She reached up and rubbed at her shoulder blade, then sighed and dropped the hand.

His gaze followed her actions. "Rough day?"

"Only usual for now. Look, I'm not sure that pursuing any kind of relationship would be wise."

"You think nothing could eventuate, then?"

She blinked, unsure why he wanted to pursue her when, clearly, she was brushing him off. "I like you a lot, Micah. But my genetic makeup and relationships are clearly inconsistent with any kind of future relationship. I have no intentions of allowing myself to either be party to such an act or to —"

He frowned, the lines of his forehead deep and slashing. Her fingers itched to rub them away. "Bullshit, Davina. You're afraid. I get that, but don't misunderstand me or think I'm some pussy."

Her mouth dropped open. No man had ever spoken to her like that before.

"I... No, I don't think you're a pussy. I think you like some, and you probably range far and wide to get what you want." Her waspish tone and the sour words hit.

His jaw tightened, as did his gaze. "You think I'm just after sex?" The words erupted like a snarl.

"Yes, I do." This time it was her voice that faltered, because she'd not only said the wrong and hurtful things to Micah, and he took the meaning as an insult. One she hadn't meant to be so blunt.

"You think little of me, don't you?" He shook his head, took a step back.

"It's not that. I don't, but to be honest, everything is against us. Work is going to shit. My family life doesn't exist, and I have no—"

He swooped in, didn't give her a chance to push him away. The lips that met hers were hard, cutting off her litany.

Davina's body turned traitor as his arms encircled her tight band that tugged her against him. They didn't move. He didn't rub or quest, simply held her in place while the heat of his flesh warmed the chill she hadn't recognised invaded her frame.

As she tugged away, he kept her close, even as she attempted to hold him at bay, her posture stiff and unresponsive.

"This means something." He rested his forehead against her. "Don't just ignore it or refuse to accept it."

"I can't." Her voice broke. "I'm too scared."

The words hung between them, a warning that she was close to the edge and one he accepted. "I know you're unsure. So am I, but both of us need whatever this promises."

A chink appeared in her psyche, tears welled, burning her eyes, and she slumped. "I don't know how," she wailed.

"We'll do it together."

He ushered her to the lounge, keeping her close; they slid to the padded seat.

Silence stretched between them. Neither willing to break the quiet communion between them, Davina thought.

Sometime around ten, Davina turned to Micah. "I haven't done any practice this week. It's been kind of a whirlwind."

"Maybe we should try, then. I've been working hard on my breathing, focus and everything." He refused to push for the moment her harder. She'd taken an important step tonight. Instead, he'd give her time to re-balance herself.

"I've, um... I set up my spare room as a meditation haven. Would you like to see it?" Her careful words sounded like the peal of bells. She was asking him to enter a place where she found herself.

"Sure, I'd love to."

He followed her across the lounge room, to a door that he'd noticed earlier was closed. As she reached out, she glanced over her shoulder. "You're the first person to see it."

His brain turned to mush, grasping exactly what she said, and didn't say.

As she opened the door, the scent of flowers wafted. The room decorated in jewel toned cushions beckoned. "It's really nice." Micah followed her into the room, noting the careful placement of the cupboard, the ambient lighting.

"I've also put in a small sound system, so I can play relaxation music. I've found that helps me to settle in."

He grinned. "Sounds like you've done a lot of thinking about this. Would you show me?"

Davina reached out, "Why don't we go one better? Even though Karly isn't here, we can still practice the techniques."

As he moved to agree, he spotted the flyers she hadn't yet checked, given they still appeared pristine. "You haven't had time to look at these?"

Her hair whipped around her face. "No time. This week has been crazy. But since you're here, maybe...?"

Ahh, now here was a problem. He could steer her towards the Kundalini which appealed viscerally, but he didn't want to give her an opportunity to later feel aggrieved that he'd set the rules between them.

Instead, he waited as she picked up the first of the flyers and read through it, screwed up her face and moved to the next. The purple flyer sat at the bottom, and her cheeks turned rosy as she skimmed it. The glazing of her eyes a clear sign of her interest and perhaps a level of arousal.

"Something interesting?" She'd given it her full attention, and at his words she jumped as if she'd forgotten he was there.

"I... Uh..."

"You've found something that appeals to you?" He knew the timbre of his voice changed, deepening. Couldn't control his own reaction to her. "Kundalini?"

"I... Yes." The breathy quality of her voice took on the strength of a siren's call.

"Perhaps you would investigate it with me?"

He waited a heartbeat, then two.

She swallowed, and he saw the movement of her throat, the way she damped her lips with the tip of her tongue. That delicate blush tracing down her neck.

"*Yessss.*"

The roar of pleasure didn't just bloom in his chest, so much as explode, radiating heat and anticipation of what they both had to look forward to. He wasn't quite ready yet to tell her what he'd placed on his bedside table. The battered and well-thumbed copy of the Kama Sutra and another, a tome on the basics of Kundalini. She wasn't ready to hear that, and he wasn't ready to explain that he felt their connection would grow through the practice of this meditation technique.

Instead, he reached out, slid a strand of hair from her face before cupping her jaw. "Thank you."

They wavered, both moving and rolling towards each other, so that they touched at chest and lips. The touch, both reverent and careful. She wasn't ready for fast and hungry, not yet. He wanted her to take his lead, to follow him into pleasure he knew lay ahead.

"Let me touch you, Davina. I want to kiss you."

Her eyes assumed the glazed look he'd seen before. "Yes. I want that."

This time, he opened his mouth, just a little, enough that his breath whispered against her flesh.

"Come closer." She sighed and complied, so that they now nestled together, while he wound his arm around her waist.

"Can you feel me, Davina? Can you feel how my heart pounds for you?"

"I... Yes." Her voice sounded strangled. His own thought processes were only held together by the briefest of threads. If he moved too fast, he'd lose control. Not now. Not tonight, he reminded himself. This was about Davina, and helping her to find not just the strong, relationship-savvy woman she could be, but also embracing the sexuality he knew lay beneath her iron-like restraints.

He stepped away and studied the woman before him, her eyes somnolent, hair tousled and totally ripe. *I want to draw her.*

He'd never felt such a strong need to draw the woman he'd been intimately involved with before, keeping both sides of himself separate as much as he could. He'd slept with Karen, but while she'd been his agent, it had been a matter of expediency. This time, it was different. There were depths and layers he wanted to explore with Davina.

"Will you take off your top for me?"

His hands mirrored her moves, shedding the cotton shirt as she uncovered herself. Her blouse dropped away, the white cotton of her bra standing out. She reached behind her back; her gaze locked on his and unhooked the clasps. The cups sagged and his mouth dried. As the scrap of material slid to the floor, he hissed with arousal.

"Your pants," Micah requested as his fingers found the clasp of his belt, loosened it, and he dealt quickly with the hook, button, and zip. He slid the pants and underwear down as she followed suit.

"This isn't quite what I had in mind." Her voice whispered in the fraught silence, and he couldn't control the rumble of a laugh.

"Maybe, but it's a hell of a way to spend time together."

He toed out of his shoes and kicked off the puddle of clothing at his ankles as she followed suit.

His body tightened as she stood there, nude in the soft lighting. He reached for her hand, shivering as their skin connected and nerves jumped. It felt like arcs of electricity raced beneath his skin as he moved closer.

Davina couldn't pull her gaze away. Micah stood before her, his hard cock engorged with desire from beneath the thatch of dark, curly hair at his centre. His face tight and flushed with a hunger that she knew was on hers, too.

God, how hungry she was for him and his body. But it was more than that. But Davina shied away from thinking about the emotional. Not now, when pleasure bloomed between them. Instead, she moved closer, so her nipples brushed against his skin. Her arousal ratcheted up another full notch, and she inhaled, his scent overwhelmingly spicy and male invaded her senses.

"I want to touch you, Micah." The words boldly tumbled from her lips before she swooped in, kissing him in hot, hungry surges, tongue tangling in the warmth of his mouth. Her hands played down his body, gripping his flanks so he'd crowd further in.

He nibbled at her neck, and she arched, form reacting instinctively as his fingers weaved magic.

Between her legs came the pulse of desire, hot and damp. She craved him in every way.

Davina reached up, tugged him to the centre of the room and the mound of cushions.

With a bold move, she sank down, pulling him along so they both reclined on the soft fabric.

"Love me, Micah."

His grin deepened. "My pleasure, my lady. Let me start with your gorgeous breasts."

Trailing his fingers along her exposed flesh until they reached the distended nubs, circled them, and Davina moaned, wanting so much more. "Suck them."

Glancing down at her, the sensuous view drugged her. His grin feral, he lapped at her skin, but refused her request. The act left her mewling, "Please."

"Not yet beautiful."

His tongue trailed down her belly toward the centre of her hunger and she writhed beneath him, wanting so much more but knowing his intentions. When he fitted his mouth between her legs, flicking at the nub of her clit, she almost screamed, her mind riding the pleasure waves that screamed through her.

"Not yet," Micah growled, but the orgasm rippled through her. It was only as she surfaced from the storm that she recognised the slide of fingers inching deep within her, and the wildness took over again. Now it was faster, the ruddy hue of his skin, the straining of his erection dictating his actions.

Davina gripped Micah by the arms and hauled him up into her body. "No. This time I want you with me."

The kiss they shared was musky with the taste of her own juices, and she dove into the carnality of their actions.

He twisted in her grasp, but she was faster, turning him over against the cushions mounded high. "I need you now, Micah. Inside me, buried deep and filling me."

He grunted as she mounted him, her legs sliding along his lean flanks, her form trembling wildly, then gave a low throaty laugh. "I aim to please, my lady."

She slid down, her body welcoming him like a glove. The sensation of fullness shattering her composure and the coil of tension spiked her pleasure. This time, her orgasm was wild, splintering her mind and soul. "Micah," she screamed, giving up control as he thrust deep. Fingers gripping her hips as he sought his own release.

When it came, he roared his pleasure, the long line of his neck exposed as he gave her every bit of himself.

Her chest shuddered; spent by the aftermath of their pleasure.

"Thank you." The whisper of breath tickled her neck as tears pricked.

Unable to speak, Davina merely nodded and cuddled in, hoping she hadn't made the biggest mistake of her life.

§

Time passed. It could have been hours or long moments as Micah lay there, spent by their wild exertions in her meditation room. His mind whirling with thoughts. He wasn't sure either of them was prepared to consider them just yet. As the night drew in, they both chilled down in the autumn evening and he spoke. "Bedroom?"

Her gaze bleary, Davina rose and took his hand, leading him out of the room and into the next. He padded behind her, checking the sway of her body, the outline of her figure and wondering not for the first time what she'd look like immortalised on canvas.

Her bedroom was spare, and he felt an echo of how she lived her life. Carefully devoid of frills and personal items.

Without a word, Micah tugged back the covers as she did on the other side of the bed and they both slid beneath them. For a moment

Davina remained still, holding herself like fragile glass that may shatter at the merest touch.

He waited, knowing she needed time, given the unfamiliarity of their situation. "You never shared this bed before, have you?"

Her head turned. "No."

"Why?"

Her gaze slid away, looking over his shoulder. Was she going to order him home? Ignore the question? Long seconds passed.

"I... They never mattered before."

He wondered if she understood just what she'd revealed and contained the smile. He could wait now, because there was no rush. In time, she'd be able to share her thoughts with him.

So, he waited, and gradually the tension in her body melted away. Her eyes closed as he waited, his arm around her shoulder nestled close, and she slept.

Their passion had clearly exhausted her, taken so much out of her, that she dozed, her head lolling slightly, and he watched, mesmerised as she slept.

As Davina snuggled in, Micah wondered if tonight was the first time she had vocalised her fear, not of rejection, but of not knowing how to love someone. Of taking the chance on a relationship.

Previously unwilling to consider such a thing, suddenly it was vitally important that he keep her close and grow whatever was between them. To teach her that love and futures didn't always end in divorce. That sometimes they could last forever, just like his parents and his brother.

Her family had let her down, and he couldn't understand how or why that had happened. How could her parents refuse to accept that their actions had caused her to fear a future and not only take responsibility but also take steps to rectify the situation? Could he be the one to make a difference in her life? He wanted that with a desperation that stole his breath, and he endured a sensation of hyperventilation that lasted long seconds.

"I'll make you understand, Davina." She snuffled, and he waited, sure for a moment she'd wake, but Davina rolled slightly and the muscles of his belly that had tightened released again. "You deserve so much more, and I'll do everything I can to make you see that. That's my promise to you."

In that moment, as the silence stretched, his arm numb from the weight of her head, truth shone like the brightest beacon. *He loved her.*

CHAPTER

EIGHT

Waking in a strange bed never put Davina in a good mood.

Waking in her own with a man was a different kettle of fish. Heart beating wildly, Davina felt sure she'd hyperventilate soon. *How did this happen?* Even as the thought bloomed, she knew she'd allowed it to happen. After a truly rotten week, where her defences were low, she'd invited him to spend the night. *I never do this!*

The sound of the shower gave her a moment to think. The bed was empty beside her, and she whispered a silent word of thanks. She scrubbed her hands over her eyes and half levered up, glanced for the alarm clock, and a heavy feeling invaded her guts. Nine o'clock. A moment of panic gripped her before rational thought took over. Saturday. It was Saturday.

At the peal of her doorbell, Davina rolled off the bed, grabbed her dressing gown from the bedroom door, and stalked toward the front of her apartment. She dragged the cotton over her nude body and cinched the belt before reaching for the door.

Elyse grinned at her, then pushed past. "Hey Dav! I'm out of coffee and thought..." Elyse's words trailed away, and Davina squeezed her eyes shut, aware of what her best friend would see.

"Umm..." Micah spoke and when Davina opened her eyes, she saw the way Elyse gawked.

"Oh. My..." A smile, sly and more than a little interested, had Davina wishing her friend far, far away. "So, you're the meditation partner?"

"You needed some coffee? I've got a jar in the cupboard." She spun quickly and retreated, passing Micah, who winked. "Gah!"

"I was just grabbing my clothes. But I'll wait in here." Micah retreated into the bedroom, shutting the door firmly as Elyse trotted behind her.

"You've been holding out on me, girlfriend."

Davina gritted her teeth. "No. He turned up and things just..." She shrugged, at a loss for words that didn't reveal her inner turmoil over the situation.

"Uh, huh. So, uh, the meditation was worthwhile, I take it? Maybe I should go join up." Every muscle in Davina's body twitched, and it took a ferocious effort on her part to release the roaring emotions.

"You can." The full jar sat to the left-hand side of the pantry and Davina snatched it out. "Now, not meaning to be rude but..."

Elyse cocked her head to one side and smiled as she accepted the bottle. "Yeah, you do. I'm a third wheel, so I'm out of here. But I'll want to talk to you later. Too much to talk about. Toodles."

Elyse sashayed down the hall, and the front door closed with a click as Davina waited, heart thudding wildly. "Of all the days," she muttered.

Micah appeared through the now opened bedroom door. "Clear?"

And now for problem number two.

"Yeah. I'll grab your things." She headed for the meditation room and collided with him. Almost falling, his hands caught her, towel slipping so his damp nakedness was only a light cotton layer from her own suddenly aroused body.

"I... uh..."

He tugged her closer, and she felt the interest that tickled her belly. "Your clothes?"

He grinned, the colour of his eyes deepening, as did the creases at the corner. "Can wait."

The kiss was leisurely, while Micah sipped at her lips Davina's will turned mush-like. When he drew away, she sighed, her mind exhausted by the sexual pleasure and the aftermath of emotions she was wholly unprepared for. "Oh, I wish..."

"What do you wish, Davina? Tell me."

A ball of sadness lodged in her chest, and while her mind screamed, *hold your tongue*, the words slipped out. "I wish life was easy and your words were promises I could rely on." She turned away, hiding the burning of her cheeks.

He caught her chin, the grip soft but compelling. "Why do you say that?"

Tears stung her eyes, and the fiery blaze of her crimson cheeks gave away her discomfiture. "Because guys say stuff in the heat of passion. Things they believe they mean, but when the crunch time comes, they know they don't, and they walk away."

"Who did that to you, Davina? Who walked away?" He gathered her close, so the wild beating of her heat echoed within him... His hard chest pillowing her form.

"I..." If only it were that simple. Her father had left. Then every one of her stepfathers. She'd seen firsthand how her mother had tried again and again.

"Davina?"

She shook her head, hoping he'd stop asking.

The tension in his body as he waited urged the words from her throat. "I've seen it. I see it every day. At work. I saw it with my father. My stepfathers. It doesn't work. They don't stay."

Now Micah vibrated, "so that's what you think of me. Here only for the bang but not—"

"No!" she screamed the words, needing him to understand the jumble inside her mind. "No, you're different, but *I'm scared*!"

His sigh echoed in the sudden quiet. "I know you're scared. Hell, I wasn't looking for more than sex either, Davina. I don't know..." Micah stopped, as if the words were stuck in his throat. "Being sure of what I want? That's hard to work out, but I do know I want the opportunity to show you how good it can be. I want you to trust me and this thing between us."

Tugging away, Davina attempted to dodge him, sliding into the room, but he followed, his very presence crowding her.

"I don't—"

"How about—"

Both spoke at the same time, and she couldn't help but goggle at the sexy naked man before her. "Please, you go first."

Micah cocked his head to the side. "Alright. How about we strike a medium? We don't talk about the deep emotions. Let's just explore the friendship with benefits option first."

Her frown must have telegraphed her distrust.

"It's not just about the sex. Actually, the sex, as great as it is, is like the cherry on top. An added benefit. But you get to know me, I get to know you..." His eyes glinted in the darkened room and Davina pondered his words.

"And if this goes nowhere?"

"We walk away. Both of us agree it was a learning experience."

She hesitated a moment longer. "And the sex?"

"Only if you want to. Only if I want to. Consenting adults, Davina."

Too good to be true, whispered her mind. Grab this opportunity with both hands, whispered another deeper part of her anatomy...

"Alright, then." Holding out her hand, she gasped as he gripped it, tugged her closer, and dropped his forehead to hers.

"We can do better than that." The whisper of his breath caressed her, and her eyes slid down, far too heavy under the sudden sensual barrage.

Their lips touched, the barest pressure. She sighed, and her mouth opened to his, welcoming the intrusion of his tongue. It slid deep as she moaned. She knew the moment his fingers found the sash around her waist before sliding up to the shoulders of the garment. He slid the cotton material off until it fell to the floor. Unheeded. Davina and Micah wound arms around each other, clinging so their bodies flowed together.

His mouth left her lips and trailed a fiery path down her neck. "Oh God, Davina. You're so bloody sexy."

She giggled at his belaboured words.

He raised his head and frowned. "What?"

"I just found that funny. Sexy but funny."

Then he flung back his head and guffawed. "Well, that kinda wrecked the mood, didn't he?" He muttered once he regained composure.

"Ha ha. Maybe we should get dressed and do something friends would do. Like find some breakfast." Her stomach trembled at the thought, yet there was an undercurrent of hopefulness threading through her veins.

His frown morphed into an assessing smile. "Sure, then afterwards I have an idea."

On a deep breath, Davina nodded. "Sure. Tell me what you have in mind?"

"Over breakfast."

CHAPTER

NINE

With careful moves, Micah swung his car into the designated space in the parking lot, well-aware that the woman beside him was nervous. "Okay there?"

She turned wide eyes on him. "I've never, umm... I've never been a date to an event like this. You're sure it's okay?"

He reached out, hand sliding over hers, thumb caressing the long fingers on her lap. "It's fine. I'm the major attraction and my date is always welcome."

Clearly unconvinced, Davina nodded, sliding her hands away from his grip. "How long have you been..."

He grinned, because this was the first time she'd asked about his profession and passion. "My first showing was ten years ago. My mother claimed my first painting was achieved when I was about a year old. She'd framed it and hung it in the hallway. Told everyone that one day it would become a collectible."

Her laugh tinkled, and he finally relaxed. "Come on. We need to get inside."

The release of the seat belt and the clunk of the door opening told him she'd followed his lead, and he rearranged his suit and tie before firmly closing the car door. She met him on the concrete at the front of the car, her ruby dress of silk lovingly fitting her form like a glove. Her black hair swept up into a chic knot at her nape, and the tiny diamond hanging from the long silver chain around her neck dipped into the hollow between her luscious breasts. The length of her legs encased in silk, but below the gown he knew lay the promise of a garter and lacy panties.

The throb of his body jerked him back to the moment he'd entered her apartment, strategically early to find her racing around, dithering about clothing choices. He'd almost called the night off and suggested a night in. The sudden honk of a car yanked him from the memory but one look at her was enough to plunge him into the well of hunger that followed him anywhere Davina was.

Her ruby red lips called like a siren, and he swayed until she reached out, hand against his chest. "You don't want the shadow of my lipstick on you, so come on big boy."

There was a playfulness in her voice he'd never heard before, and it filled some unknown emptiness in his chest. "Only because I'm going to kiss it off you later, then unwrap you like a Christmas present."

"Promises, promises," she snickered, as he slid her hand into the crook of his elbow.

"Stick with me, and I'll show you a good time." His Humphrey Bogart was atrocious, but she laughed.

In his mind, he vowed one day he'd paint her. But this painting would be for him alone. But now wasn't the time to think about the setting and lighting. Tonight, was the opening of his latest showing and at the door, looking for him, was Karen.

People packed the room of the gallery. The wine in the glass that she clutched with numb fingers had long since warmed.

Men and women crowded around Micah, and she took a moment to examine him in his element. His hands moved expressively, fully immersed in discussing brush strokes or pigments, she guessed. Every now and again, he'd look up, grab her gaze with his and smile apologetically.

Her heels didn't click as she turned, her eyes seeking the painting that caught her attention. A seascape, very like the one he'd painted and now hung in her lounge. Only this one was a day-scape, alive with colour and movement.

"He's exceptional, Davina."

Karen, his assistant, crowded in beside her. "I've got the night version of that one in my lounge."

"He painted the night version the week after his mother's funeral, you know. When he moved home. I remember telling him it was dark and moody, and he turned to me and said it reflected where he was. The flecks of colour and stars were the hope for the future. The roiling seas, his emotions. He's an instinctive artist."

"He's also fantastic and there's a lot of them already sold, if the stickers are anything to go by."

Karen giggled. "True. His work is highly collectible."

Davina couldn't help her tiny snicker. "He said his mother kept his first picture."

"Really?" There was an odd inflection in Micah's agent's voice. "He never told me that."

"Oh. Well, uh, how long have you been with him?"

"We've known each other for years, but I've been his agent for the last eight. Apart from that, we were together for about the last two... two-and-a-half years."

That stilled Davina, her heart plunging to her guts.

"Oh, I didn't realise."

"It was mutually convenient. Neither of us wanted anything, you know, permanent. But it's over and has been for a while. Look, I don't know you, but he's the happiest I've seen him in a long time."

Davina took a half step back, looked critically at the woman in front of her and gave a smile she doubted reached her eyes. "Yeah. Look, I'm not feeling all that well. Could you make my farewells to Micah?" The bubble she'd been ignoring all night, the one lodged in her chest, swelled, cutting off the supply of oxygen to her brain. Dots of dark bounced in front of her gaze. Then she turned and stumbled forward, thankful no one blocked her way.

"I..." The heat of the room became oppressive as she turned. After several rapid blinks, Davina spied the nearest waiter and dumped the drink on her tray.

At the door a warm hand curved over hers on the handle. "What's wrong?"

She shivered despite the heat. Her insides chilled as Micah increased the pressure on her fingers. "Nothing. I mean, I've got a headache and I need to go home."

"Davina?"

Her name stopped her in her tracks. "Look, I'm not sure this is going to work. I... Karen is exceptional." That slipped out along with a tear, and his sigh ricocheted through her mind.

"Karen. Right." Carefully, Micah spun her in his direction. "What did she say?"

"That you'd been intimate. That it was over." Setting her gaze at a point over his shoulder, Davina sought to ignore the flare of frustration on his face and the knowledge emblazoned in his sapphire blue eyes.

"So, what's the problem?"

Was he genuinely unknowing, or was it an act? "Look, even though it's over between the two of you, it's got to be uncomfortable. Your association is long standing and business so—"

"It's done, Davina. We're great friends. Would you hold that against me? I love Karen like a sister, and I would protect her, but with you, it's different. *Please.* Don't leave. I promise, we can talk after this is over."

On one hand, she felt mean and small feeling like this, but the ground beneath her feet was pretty damned slippery. She'd already broken all the rules she'd had surrounding relationships and men for Micah. It wouldn't take much for everything to come down on her.

Yet the thought of just leaving almost tore her in two. "For now. But we talk after." Her voice sounded raw, but she knew the instant her words settled in his brain. The lines of strain around his mouth softened a little.

"Good. We'll talk after."

He got through the event, tense and on edge. Yet Micah took great pains to ensure Davina had company. His sister and brothers didn't ask why he'd insinuated her into the middle of the gang when he had to go on stage. They just welcomed her.

No one questioned her presence, though there was a decided twinkle in Miriam's eye. He avoided talking to her tonight, but knew tomorrow she'd demand her pound of flesh and answers. He wasn't yet sure how that would pan out.

The evening drew to a close, and Micah ushered Davina to the car. "I hope that wasn't too much for you."

She perched in her seat; hands gripped together as she looked him in the eye. "I acted like a child earlier, Micah, and should have respected you and the situation with Karen. I'm sorry."

Unable to stop himself, Micah reached out and cupped her cheek, pulling her towards him. "You did nothing wrong. With your family situation, it's not the sort of thing you'd have experience with. Mind you, our arrangement wasn't exactly normal by most people's standards. I should have told you about her beforehand and that while we are still friends, there is no anger or..." Searching for the right words had never seemed so hard before.

"Micah—"

"I should have been upfront, so you weren't blind-sided. I'm sorry too." He kissed her. Kept it gentle so as not to spook her, then retreated to let her recover herself.

"Can you... Can you stay?" The hesitancy in her words gouged him.

"I can, but I need some clothes. Mind if we drop by the house?" He didn't live far from here, and at her nod, he fastened his seatbelt, then left the carpark. They drove in silence, two people lost in their own thoughts. At his place, he gave a quick, "I'll only be a moment or two," and dashed inside. On a whim, he hurried to his studio and grabbed pencils and a small sketch pad. In his bedroom, he grabbed two sets of clothes, basic toiletries, and the charger for his phone and shoved them into a small overnight bag he kept on top of his wardrobe. "Everything else can wait."

Once he returned to the car, he slid the bag onto the back seat and reversed out of the driveway. Spying a small all-hour mall, he pulled the vehicle into the parking lot. "I'll be back in a moment."

With his wallet in his hand, he moved quickly, heading for the grocery store, his mind urging him to purchase the small number of supplies that he was sure would help ease the discussion that lay ahead.

Returning to the car again, he watched as Davina caught sight of his shopping bags. "What have you bought?"

He grinned. "I'll explain once we get back to your place." He deposited the bags on the back seat, along with his bag, and climbed into the car. "Let's go."

This time, he felt more assured as they parked in the complex, his car filling the second slot allocated to her apartment.

He grabbed his bag and the shopping before she could offer and followed her to the entrance, waited as she unlocked the security gates to the residential zone and followed her to the front door.

In the kitchen, he unloaded the bags and swiftly cleared up, then dropped his bag into her bedroom. Neither speaking even though they both knew there'd been a major shift in their relationship.

He waited, perched on the bed as she self-consciously shucked the dress. When her fingers moved to undo the stockings, he stood and stilled her fingers. "Leave them on for now." Through the mirror, he noted the shake of her fingers and the shock in her eyes.

"Okay."

Instead, Micah reached for the light satin wrap he'd spied and assisted her to slide into it. "I need to take off the makeup." She retreated to the bathroom, and he moved to the kitchen to prepare the setting.

On a plate he arranged strawberries and the small Belgian chocolates, poured two glasses of champagne into the flutes he found and carried everything to the lounge and set up the coffee table.

"Oh..." Her surprise was genuine, her smile tremulous. "What... Where did you get... At the supermarket?" He nodded and retreated to fetch the last item. A small posy of flowers. Not roses, because they were too cliché in his mind. Instead, he'd found a small bunch of yellow, red and orange tulips. He remembered his father getting them for his mother every year on her birthday, commenting that they meant love and devotion.

"Micah!"

He pushed them into her hands, pleased at the tiny gasp she gifted him with. "Flowers for a beautiful lady."

She scurried off, likely looking for a vase, he guessed, and returned with a smile, placing the bunch now in a cut crystal holder on the coffee table. "No one has ever done this for me." She glanced up, and he noted tiny shimmering tears on her lashes. He ached for her, and would have reached out to wipe them away, but Davina shook her head. "No. Why, Micah? Why did you do this?"

"Because I want you to understand that I value you, Davina."

"But isn't this just about sex?"

He waited for the jolt to his gut to pass, taking the minute to accept what she was really asking. "I'm not after just sex Davina." Frustration, that she didn't understand and couldn't see past her own history, speared him and he thrust his hands into his hair, spun in a circle while keeping his mouth closed. He needed to contain himself before the pressure in his skull burst. *Inhale. Exhale.* Just like Karly taught you, he instructed himself. Control your reaction, slow your breathing. Once more, finding his equilibrium, he turned back to Davina. "Look, maybe we need to halt the sex for a while? Let's just be friends. We can continue to practice together—"

"Practice what? Basic meditation? Kundalini or—"

"Maybe I should go. Give you time to settle."

"Maybe you should." Tears glinted in her eyes while her mouth twisted into a mulish twist.

His heart battered and somewhat torn, screamed it was time to leave and save himself from grief. His brain entreated him to wait. To see that the anger on her face was merely a facade of bravado. He read people and painted them for a living and surely, he could see through this too.

Micah already had his hand on the door. Unconsciously, he'd moved, protective instincts working in overdrive.

He looked down, stunned. Slid his hand from the metal knob. "No."

His turn was slow and measured.

Her eyes widened.

"No. I'm not going."

Her lips quivered.

"You need me. I'm staying."

CHAPTER

TEN

Monday morning, Davina rolled out of bed. The suit she'd chosen the night before hanging on the door of her closet, along with the blouse and shoes. On her dressing table, neatly folded, were underwear and stockings.

A dash into the shower and back did little to clear the wisps of fog from her mind or warm her up. The chill remaining from her altercation with Micah the day before, and her stomach clenched hard. Nausea rose, but she beat it back.

"Forget him."

It didn't help, though. Memories of hurling angry words at him before pushing him out the door continued to play on a reel to reel inside her mind.

With ruthless efficiency, she set about dressing. Applied her makeup and fastened her hair into a tight and restrictive knot.

Snatching up her bag, already packed with files and her work laptop, she reached for her keys and started running through her schedule in her mind. Seven thirty senior staff meeting. Eight, meet new PA. Eight thirty, first clients of the day and thereafter at twenty-minute intervals until eleven and first court appearance of the day. Return to office by four in time for briefing of new clients, paperwork and so on. "Just an average day."

The car started on time, and she glanced at the clock on the console. Six-thirty, time for her commute. Grab a coffee and check emails before the first meeting.

Only Jim and Adele, the receptionist, were there before her and she nodded at both on the way to her office, opened the door and stilled. Shock stealing her breath and her mouth dropped open.

On the desk sat an enormous bunch of tulips. Red, gold and yellow.

The ache in her chest bloomed, and she backed away, gaze glued to the magnificent display on her desk. Adele came scampering around the corner. "They arrived just before you did. Aren't they gorgeous?"

At a loss to know how to respond, Davina gave a jerky nod.

"Who are they from?" Adele crowded in, and it took precious seconds for Davina's mind to process the question.

"A friend."

Adele snickered. "If I had a friend who sent me flowers like that, they'd likely get lucky. As in often."

Unable to speak, thoughts and impressions zooming through her mind like cars on a racetrack, Davina advanced on the desk. She touched one bloom, then another.

"There wasn't a note, so I thought for sure you'd know who they were from. The courier was waiting outside the door when I arrived."

Suddenly, it was all too much. The need for silence and privacy overcame the fog and moved. "Thanks Adele. I can take it from here." Davina waited for the door to close with a click before she rounded the desk and slumped into her chair. "*Why, Micah?*"

There was no answer. Lifting her hand to rub at aching and tired eyes, Davina realised she still held her bag. She sighed, a long echo of sound. "I need to work."

So, with little enthusiasm, Davina hefted the bag and retrieved the laptop and files. Work had always fixed everything before and would again now.

CHAPTER

ELEVEN

Micah scrutinised his work. "Shit," he declared, and grappled the canvas from the stand. It was garbage, just like most of the pieces he'd started and discarded in the last few days. The urgency that drove him right now was centred around the one thing he couldn't have. The woman who refused to answer his calls, who hadn't turned up at meditation and hadn't acknowledged his flowers.

He hadn't taken her for a quitter. *And yet, she's dodging you.*

The pull to work with the sketch he'd completed he'd but so far ignored, at the back of his pad, called. With a huff, he stalked to the table where he'd left it, tore through the pages until the back one, Davina, was before him.

His fingers itched to trace the lines he'd engraved on the page.

Do it, his heart urged.

"I shouldn't. I should close this up and ignore it." He couldn't, though.

Urgency vibrated. Without thinking, he reached for a large, prepped canvas, fitted it to the painting stand. Tore the page from

87

the book and taped it to the corner. "I've got to get her out of my head."

He wiped his fingers carefully on the old rag lying beside the chalk sticks, imagined in his mind the strokes and colours, the shading and textures.

He reached over and began.

❧

Three weeks had passed since Davina had pushed Micah from her unit. Three weeks where she'd wallowed and worked herself to exhaustion until she fell into bed at night. Not that she didn't think about him. She did. Every day, he was there in her memories. Either looking at the artwork in her lounge or lying in her bed.

Every time her phone rang, she'd checked the number. He'd tried in the first week every day. Driving into her car spot, she spied the place where he'd parked. At the door, she remembered his indulgent smile, waiting for her to open the door.

At work, Adele had enquired casually a time or two about 'Mr. Flowers', as she'd dubbed him.

The longer she stayed away from Micah, the more she ached.

Every night was a replay of their time together. The good, the fucking exceptional, and the horrible way she'd ended it.

Elyse rang and asked what was happening. Davina prevaricated, unwilling to admit to her friend exactly what she'd done.

Her mother returned from Bali, new husband in tow and gushing about the great time she'd had. Not once had she noted that Davina was low. Davina endured a quick restaurant meal with the happy couple, then decamped, unable to be around people clearly besotted with each other.

Laura called with a baby update and news from her half-siblings. From her father, nothing. She had expected nothing else.

Life passed by in a slow and painful blur.

"I don't need a man," she whispered. True, she didn't need *any* man. She *needed* Micah. Tears welled, and she scrubbed at her face. "I need to get out of this mood." She clambered from the bed, well-aware that moping would only lead to worse things.

The envelope which arrived yesterday from him waited on her dresser. Her eyes settled on it. Her fingers itched to open it.

Instead, she whirled and headed for the bathroom. A quick shower refreshed her somewhat, and she tugged on comfortable jogging pants and a matching top. Perhaps some vigorous exercise would help take her mind off *him.*

It was only a matter of minutes. Key and card shoved in the tiny zip up pocket of her pants, phone stuffed into a small waistband carrier. She hit the road, moving fast. Trying to outrun her demons, to numb her body and suppress the urge to ring Micah.

The sultry weather closed around her like a thick, oppressive glove. Sweat poured over her skin. Muscles burned in anguish, tested to their limits in the now unfamiliar rhythm and exertion.

Into mile three, she slowed to a jog, followed by a walk, exhausted, and every muscle trembled as she entered a local coffee shop zone. Davina hunched over as she gave into her lungs need for oxygen. Breathing deeply until the shudders and bellowing of her chest passed.

Rehydrate, she told her body.

Entering the first small shop, she moved to the fridge, reached for a bottle of coconut water. The cool air flowed over her sticky body, and she shivered. A hand reached past her and grabbed a cold green tea.

"Don't get too cold, your muscles will seize."

Micah.

"I... Uh, nice to see you, Micah." She turned, cursing her bad luck at looking sweaty when they met again. She closed the door, wishing the ground would just swallow her here and now.

"You cancelled your classes with Karly. Why?"

Feeling like a deer under headlights, Davina ducked her head and moved to the counter. "Umm work and stuff."

She paid for her drink, and aware Micah would simply follow if she left, Davina waited, her stomach a mass of knots. *How can I explain without sounding foolish?*

He joined her outside, and they found a table with a pair of wrought-iron seats. She sank down gratefully, her mind whirling.

"Davina?"

She moistened her lips. "Because it terrified me." Davina angled her head away, so he wouldn't see the turmoil and regret in her eyes. "I said some pretty unconscionable things to you, Micah. I mean, you said you weren't just in it for the sex and I pushed and prodded. I made you out to be the bad guy. You didn't deserve that, and I need you to understand I spend so much time in my head, I just..." Davina swiped at the lock of hair that broke loose from its confinement. When she looked at him now, she had to bite her lip hard, teeth pressing down on unprotected flesh. "I was so wrong, and I let my fears cloud my judgement. You didn't deserve any of the nastiness I heaped on you."

His grave look had her stomach churning. "No, I didn't. But I also understand you're hurting."

"Ha! You're far too kind to me. I don't deserve you cutting me a break. I was rude and awful when I had absolutely no reason to act like I did."

He reached out, his hand sliding over the one she held her drink in. "I knew about your family. You'd told me. It's why I gave you space, but Davina, you can't keep running from your past. You have to face it. Talk to them and find a path forward."

Now Davina laughed. "You sound like Karly!"

"I've been taking some private lessons and talking to her a bit. I'm really keen to learn more. But Davina? I'd love to share that with you."

The burn of pleasure scoured her. Washed over her. She closed her eyes as the thud of her heart increased. "I... I want that too, Micah."

"Then let me take you home."

She felt the tug of his hands, her lids raising as she noted the flare of heat in his gaze. "Yes. Yes, I will."

Unsure where the next encounter would lead them, Micah ushered Davina to the vehicle. She climbed in, apologising for her appearance.

Her cheeks rosy, her hair wild, but there was a definite sparkle in her eyes. One he hadn't seen before.

The last three weeks had been hell. The more he tried to contact her, the harder she'd shut him out. He'd sent flowers, but she hadn't acknowledged them.

He noted the lines of strain around her eyes, and the unmistakable truth was she'd also lost weight. She wasn't big by anyone's stretch, so the lost pounds were more than noticeable.

The silence stretched as he drove in the gate and parked beside her vehicle. Without a word, they climbed out. He locked it and watched as she pushed the button to close the gate behind them. Then they entered the residential area.

At her door, he waited as she shoved the key in the lock.

As Davina glanced over her shoulder, he saw concern. "Look, I don't have to come in."

"Please. I'd like to talk, you know." She half shrugged and pushed in through the opening, so he followed her through to the lounge, the door closing behind him.

Davina hovered. "Would you like a drink?"

He didn't really, but clearly she needed something to occupy herself, given she didn't settle in the chair near him.

Micah waited for her to return, a glass in each hand. She handed one over, then moved to the far end, and settled in the seat.

"What would you like to discuss?"

"I'm wanting to continue learning about meditation and the kundalini bit intrigues me. So, I did some reading—" and here Davina turned crimson, and it took great pains to hold the smile at bay. "I need someone to practice with, and I don't feel comfortable asking anyone else. I mean…" Her hands twisted in the air; agitation palpable. "Look, I started this journey with you and to be honest—"

"Always the best policy," he interjected.

"Yeah… Look, I like you. I'm attracted to you and find you sexually satisfying and…" Davina shook her head. "I'm making a hash of this," she muttered.

"You enjoy sex with me?"

At his blunt comment, she blinked, then nodded. "Yes. You're sexy and strong and I feel safe when you touch me."

A seismic shift took place inside his chest. It wasn't a protestation of love, but it was a gigantic step for her. He doubted she ever admitted this to anyone else.

"And how do you see this progressing, Davina?"

She reached out, took a deep drink of her water as quiet settled over the room. Micah waited. He could afford to be patient. Even more, he refused to lead her along, then have her cry he'd coerced her. If he wanted an all-in partnership, she'd have to come to terms with it herself.

"I… I'm not sure I want to learn more about meditation from Karly. I'm thinking we could investigate it together. I found…" here Davina cleared her throat, the crimson of her face deepening. "On the internet there're these tutorials. And books. But I'm not sure I'm really comfortable with someone directing…"

"Ah. Yes, Karly and I discussed that. She said some proponents of Kundalini don't like external direction and prefer to practice away from others. That they see it as a form of private meditation and growth. She's suggested some books we might find useful. Or me. I didn't discuss you." It was important that she realised he would betray nothing, she said.

"Alright, so books?"

"And videos."

Davina's face flamed.

"I'm not into pornography and—"

He sputtered, aware that his face probably mirrored his surprise. "It's not pornography. It's actually someone discussing various aspects of the meditative side. She's talking and offering poses and information with lifelike dolls. It involved no humans, apart from the presenter in the clips I watched."

"Oh...," Davina blinked.

He found her confusion endearing. His brain urged him to be cautious with Davina right now, while he simply wanted to reach out and .... "Davina, can I touch you?"

Her slow nod spurred him forward. He moved, shifted to the seat next to her. Every move careful so as not to spook her.

A heartbeat and a second passed.

He moved one hand, bringing it to rest on her knee.

Nerves quivered beneath his careful touch, but he stilled his fingers, waiting for the reaction to pass, all the while hoping the rapid tattoo in his chest would settle.

"Uh, Micah? Would you come with me?"

She slid his hand away, rose, then reached out to him. Her eyes beckoned and, unable to say no, he followed her to the meditation room.

In the doorway, he stilled, unsure what would happen next. She slipped off her top and leggings, so only a thin layer of cotton covered her.

His Adam's apple bobbed as he swallowed, belly aflame with sudden hunger. His mouth dry and his lips... He licked them, hunger roaring.

With slow graceful moves, Davina dropped to the mound of cushions. "Get comfortable."

Fingers fumbled with his belt as he toed out of his shoes. *Socks can wait.* Micah's jeans hit the floor with a thud, and he shrugged off his shirt. Naked apart from silky boxers, he settled into the basic position while his gaze settled on her face.

"We should breathe." Her eyes entreated something from him. If only he knew what it was.

With an aching chest, he closed his eyes, inwardly groping for the centre that would balance him.

In and out. Hear, feel, taste… Every effort sank into finding the peace he'd now come to associate with his meditative practices.

With every breath, he felt the movement of his chest, the way it welcomed the oxygen into his lungs and expelled the carbon dioxide, his mind slowing from the raging pace. Now he noted the sound of her breaths, the scent of her.

It felt *right.*

Firmly settling himself, he opened his eyes. Davina's gaze settled on his.

"Let me try something," he croaked, and Davina blinked.

"Yes."

Without jerking, he scootched forward, moving over the mound of pillows until he was opposite her, then extended his legs so they were bracketing her body.

Davina frowned.

"Open your legs and slide them over mine."

It took a moment as she fidgeted but complied.

Afraid he'd scared her, he whispered, "simply breathe."

Once more, they concentrated until his need settled. Now, when he opened his eyes, he pressed his hand against his chest. "My heart beats." He felt the thud and revelled in the feeling of being alive.

Now he reached out for her. "Place your hand where mine was. Feel the way my heart beats for you." He settled his hand over her heart. "Close your eyes and feel the connection."

His beat settled into a rhythm in synch with hers.

They stayed like that for long moments, simple communion between them deepening the bond between them.

When she pulled away, her gaze roamed his face. "That was… amazing."

"There's a lot more. That one is purely to help us harmonise. Karly gave me a list of a couple of introductory things to work on until we find our way forward."

"And it's not all about sex, is it? It's about learning to be together in harmony. I guess I didn't really think about that when I first signed up to the lessons."

He couldn't help quirking an eyebrow. "Really?"

Davina snickered. "Were you looking for anything else?"

"Really? No. What I didn't realise is that I'd meet you. That I'd want more and that the practice would become a new cornerstone in my life."

She rose. "How about I go make tea and change? I'd really like to learn more about what you were looking for and what you've got out of it so far."

"Better yet, how about I make the tea? You go change or whatever and by the time you're done, we'll be ready."

TWELVE

Davina didn't exactly plan to take forever changing, she just vacillated after a quick shower. Leggings were comfortable, but jeans like him made sense. Did she wear a loose blouse or t-shirt? In the end, with a growl, she grabbed the leggings and oversize tunic and shoved them over her underwear.

Isn't it funny I didn't feel the least bit embarrassed about stripping down in front of him?

The thought flashed through her mind, and she bit her lip firmly. "Don't go overthinking, Davina. It's how you got yourself in trouble before."

Tossing her clothes into the hamper, she flung open the door and wandered to the table Micah had set with cups, teapot and some biscuits. She couldn't control her grin, realising he'd found her secret stash of jammy shortbreads.

With a sigh, Davina dropped into a seat. "So…"

"How's everything going at work? I know you were having assistant problems."

"Ah. A new one started, and she looks like she'll work out for me.

I um, I'm thinking of taking some time off, though. I need to do some re-evaluating of my life."

"When?"

She licked her lips. "I thought maybe in two weeks. I was going to call you. Talk to you. Apologise again, because I was awful." She picked up a teaspoon, scooped some sugar into her cup and poured the tea, then realised she'd done it the wrong way around and sighed. "I shouldn't have accused you of lying. It was more than unfair, and I know you were honest all the way along. I guess, I got scared and was trying to get rid of you before I could get involved."

Davina shrugged.

Micah remained quiet, as if aware she needed to say the words before she could dodge them again.

"I'm not good with people getting close. I started down the meditation path because I was looking for someone who'd—I guess —scratch the itch."

"And now?"

Her gaze slid away from his. "I really don't know. That's part of my problem, because I'm confused, Micah. I've got to change, but I don't know how."

She picked up her tea, sipped, and tried to sort through the tangled mass of thoughts in her brain.

"You pushed me away." His words stung, but he soothed the comment by reaching out, rubbing his hand over hers, and Davina sighed.

"I did. I'm not proud of it." Shaking her head, she tried to push forward. "I want to investigate this, whatever it is, with you. I need someone who'll make sure I'm accountable and don't slide back into my shell."

"And you feel safe with me?"

"Well, yes and no. I mean, I feel safe that we can explore the tantric practices together. That you won't push me to do something I'm not comfortable with." *This conversation is so damned difficult. He's prodding me, expecting me to talk about my fears!*

"And?"

"And what?"

"So why don't you feel safe with me at the same time?"

She grinned for a moment, watched as he blinked in response, then worried her lip. "You make me think of and want more. I'd decided that family and entanglements weren't my thing. Based on my experience with my parents, as I explained. Then my work seemed to compound it. But since I met you, I don't know. It's like I realise there is more than just the physical side between us. My mother always used to drone on about needing a man. I always thought it was for the sexual gratification part, see? But I *feel* with you. That scares me the most."

Micah moved, slid off his chair, and rounded the table. She turned to him as he gathered her into a hug. The gentle caress of his hands up and down her back had the stiffness she hadn't even registered about her body wash away. "It scares me, but I want to know more. Will you give me another go?"

His laugh was a bark of sheer joy that wobbled again her, as her face nestled against his stomach.

"I'll do more than give you another go. I'll take you home with me, if you'll let me."

Oh, man! He was hurrying, and the constant fear of relying on him enveloped her. "Well, maybe not today, but I'd like that. In the future."

He stepped away with a wink. "Of course. In the future."

CHAPTER

THIRTEEN

Micah put the finishing touches on the table, knowing she'd be here soon. He'd cleaned up the area he'd kept for his meditation room, changed the sheets on the bed, and even cleaned the bathroom.

The chicken taco chilli was cooking in the slow cooker his sister had given him last Christmas. He had strawberry mousse on ice and champagne in the fridge. The table he'd draped in white linen and added tulips, the black plate set balancing it all with the silverware shining. His mother would be proud of him, he thought with a grin.

Sliding over to the small stereo, he chose a piece subtle enough to be romantic, but not so much that she'd take fright.

The phone trilled in his pocket. His sister. "Hello?"

"How's the dinner going? Turned it down yet?"

Rolling his eyes, he checked the pot. "Yes."

"Good. Did you put clean towels in the bathroom?"

That stopped him dead. "No."

"Honestly Micah, do it now. If you're going all out to impress her, don't forget the minor stuff. Dessert?"

"Cooling."

"What about—"

"I gotta go, Sis. She'll be here any moment and I need to fix the towels." With that, he cut the line and headed to the bathroom. *Change the towels and stop over thinking everything.*

Once more back in the lounge he waited, nervous that she'd not turn up, even though she'd promised. He understood her fears now, not that he expected her to not turn up, but still...

In the newly decked out meditation retreat, he'd placed cushions, deep and mounded for comfort, laid in supplies of incense and a music tower to play suitable tunes. He'd set up a bookstand with titles that would enhance their practices. The lights were set to dim. It was all in readiness.

At the peal of the doorbell, his stomach lurched. He was at the door in several strides, swinging it open.

There she stood, hair in a plait over her shoulder. Her eyes glinted in the early evening light. She'd dressed in simple black yoga pants with a close-fitting crop top. "I brought some wine," she muttered as he leaned in for a kiss.

"In a moment." Their lips met, clung, and the balloon of worry in his chest melted away. "Come inside."

"Oh, whatever you've got cooking smells divine."

He laughed. "It's usually the woman cooking, but it's a simple Chicken Taco Chilli. I thought something easy would be best. Then we can focus on the meditation."

"You're right. I brought my bag like you said." She indicated to the duffle on the stoop beside her and he ushered her in, reaching for the bag and swinging it up.

"I'll pop it in the bedroom." They'd both decided that they were adult enough to share a bed, even if there was no sex.

She followed him. "I didn't really check this room out last time."

Micah waited, let her take in the dark room, the heavy furnishings and carvings of his bed head. "It's very, ah, erotic. Sensual. I should have guessed. You're a sensual man."

He wasn't totally sure if that was a compliment, which must have shown on his face.

"I mean, you're a pastellist, and you've got this kind of loose way of moving. You're an amazing lover and—"

He couldn't help the action that followed. Swooping in and catching her close for a deep and not-quite-satisfying kiss. Lips and teeth moved in concert with his hands, roaming over the planes of her body.

He trembled with pent up desire when they finally tugged away.

"Well, that was fun." Her face flushed and voice husky affected regions of erogenous zones he desperately tried to ignore, yet the twitch of his cock told him he failed.

Instead of giving in to the hunger, he twined his fingers around hers. "Come, let me feed your body then feed your soul."

She followed, and he urged her to sit while he scooped up the bowls. "I'll serve and be out in a moment."

"Something I can help with?" she called to his retreating back.

"Yeah, stay where you are."

She laughed, and he realised it was the first time he'd heard her laugh freely.

Micah took a moment, gripping onto the bench to relax muscles and regain his senses. If he didn't, he'd make a move too stupid to be borne. She needed to be treated carefully, like fragile china, not ploughed without thought, he reminded himself.

Once again in control of himself, he ladled the chilli into bowls, reached for the thick hunks of bread he'd prepared earlier and carried them to the table on a tray. He'd also included small bowls with grated cheese and sour cream.

"Garnishes, bread and chilli."

"This looks fantastic." Davina's eyes settled on the cream. "I think I'll just add a bit of this." She scooped it up and placed it atop her bowl.

He grabbed the same, and they settled in to eat wordlessly.

Once her bowl was empty, she leaned into the back of her seat.

"You're an amazingly wonderful cook. I'm okay with the basics, thanks to Home Economics but this is way out of my comfort zone."

He cleared the bowls and utensils away. "It's rather simple actually. But now for a tough question. Dessert now or later?"

Davina rubbed her stomach. "Later, I think. We should probably talk about tonight's practice. What do you have in mind?"

"Let me get this lot in the dishwasher and I'll show you what I've found."

He disappeared into the kitchen and rinsed, then loaded the machine. Tonight, he hoped she'd be willing to try something different. To delve deeper into their tantric practices.

The book he'd planned to show her waiting just inside the meditation room.

He'd bought a pillow book, and the Kama Sutra in all seven volumes, but the latter he might hold off until later, he thought.

When he headed back to the lounge, she was at the door of his meditation room.

He gulped, for the first time unsure how she'd take what else awaited inside.

"I should warn you, I, uh, may have taken a liberty."

"It's okay. Show me."

He pushed the door open and waited for her gaze to settle on the artwork he'd hung.

Davina. Her skin glowing in the lamplight, breasts full and high. Her dark hair pooling over a pillow.

"You... Oh my God, you painted me." She advanced slowly towards the image, and he waited, not sure what her reaction would be. "I'm uh, naked. Well, waist up anyway, but the way you painted it..."

It was almost too much to wait, to let her pass judgement, but the need to hear her, to seek her approval, rode him hard.

"It's amazing."

He released the breath he held. "You like it?"

She whirled, launched herself at him. "Like it? It's bloody amazing. But why? I mean, I don't look that way—"

"You do. When you orgasm, you almost shine. Your eyes close and you push back, hard. Your hair cascades over the pillows like liquid silk and your breasts are firm and supple while your body milks mine. You're like some ancient goddess and I... This is the you I see when you come apart for me."

Davina's eyes shone. "Just one request. This is only for you and me, right?" Her laugh sounded shaky, and he understood. It was intimate and personal.

Micah cupped her face, his hands unsteady. "For our eyes only."

"Okay. Even so, wow."

Davina knew the moment something changed deep inside her. Coming face-to-face with the painting he'd done of her, from memory invoked a response that left her amazed and humbled.

Even now, after the first surprising flash of amazement passed, she had to keep looking, to remind herself that was her!

They each took a moment, shaking their bodies to prepare for the meditative practices that lay ahead. In her mind, she heard the admonition to breathe, to fill her lungs fully, then empty them. To find that centred inner space.

Relaxed and ready to begin, Davina turned toward Micah, aware he'd also found his balance.

Micah reached for a book he'd placed on the cupboard by the door, several colourful tags noting pages he'd planned to return to. "I know I said this wasn't about sex, but we've been back together practicing for a couple of weeks. It's why I asked you to stay over, especially given you're now on leave. I'd like to take things a little further?"

He reached for the loose shirt he wore and shucked it. "The books

I was reading before talked about the importance of trust. I need to ask you, do you trust me, Davina?"

The words speared her. "Yes, Micah I do. You're meaning to go to the next level, right?"

Her gaze wavered, just for an instant. He was asking her to show her trust. With a firm movement, she removed the crop top, well-aware that this time they'd move deeper into the web.

Her breasts, released from their confinement, sagged.

He smiled. "More?"

In concert they finished disrobing until they stood naked, bodies limned by the candlelight. Micah pressed the button and music they moved in close, body to body. "Feel my breath, the way it shares my spirit," he whispered against her lips, and she revelled in the way she responded.

"Feel my breath against your skin. The way it energises me."

Their gazes meshed as her belly quivered in response. Long moments of intensity passed, her body a mass of quivering nerve endings that jumped and flared with each successive movement of her diaphragm.

Now he sank to the floor, and she followed, settling herself in his lap. The intimacy deeper than previously experienced as skin lay naked against skin.

Her breath caught again, and it took every ounce of willpower to push past the inherent arousal as his their bodies nestled intimately together.

She dug deep, looking for her balance, until finally it flared. *Breathe... Hold it in, let it go. Just be.*

The rhythm soothed her.

Sooner than she would have liked. They pulled away from the sacred position and stood. He held her close, so their bodies meshed again, nipples scraping against his hard chest.

Closing her eyes only increased the awareness of their joint nakedness. "Look at me," Micah requested.

"That's the woman I painted," he whispered against her ear, and she slowly turned her head toward him. "Relaxed and sated. Heavy, somnolent eyes with sheened skin."

This time, when his hands slid over her skin, it was totally sexual, though leaving her with the wordless understanding that she could pull away. Refuse his advances.

"It's so amazing."

"So, let me paint all of you. For me and no one else."

The request ricocheted through her mind. It would demand that she totally strip herself bare for him, in a way she hadn't yet done. And yet, the thought tugged deeply at her psyche.

"I..." *God, for the first time, I want to say yes. To be totally bare for him.* "Yes."

He grinned. "Thank you."

Now he moved in, the kiss light and testing. She increased it with lips, eager to open for him. His tongue glanced against hers, redolent with his own taste, deep and musky.

Davina's hands curved over his shoulders, glorying in the strength sheathed in his silky skin, while his own curved around her waist.

The length of his cock, now upwardly thrusting, jutted against her belly, and the lips of her sex quivered in a surge of sudden and powerful need.

"Fuck me, Micah. Fuck me now. Hard and fast."

Her heartbeat raced, but he lifted her into his arms.

"Bed. I want to lavish everything on you. I want to feast on you until you scream in my arms." Micah carried her to the bedroom, nudging at the door with his hip before reverentially laying her on the counterpane. Her gaze followed his movements as he reached for the top draw and the foil packet which he tore open.

He handed the tiny latex item in her hand. "Please."

In that moment, she welcomed everything and anything he gave her. Placing the item at the tip of his engorged penis, she rolled it over, but before she could lie back, he lifted her again onto his steely cock, settled on the bed with her clinging with arms and legs.

"You want me to fuck you?" The rough words excited her as much as their meditation had both soothed and aroused.

"Please." She knew her body was ready, already moist and hungry for his invasion.

He shoved hard, deep inside her, in a sudden movement.

Davina keened with pleasure at the sudden sensation of fullness. Unable to stop, she threw herself against his arm, arching and demanding more, lost in the throes of impossible desire.

With hands gripping tight, she met his thrusts, the damp friction deep inside her body, the movement of breast to chest igniting a primal chain reaction.

"So beautiful," he muttered as she writhed in his grasp.

"More, Micah, more," she chanted, urging him to go faster, wilder movements as the bed groaned under the sudden frenzied action.

Between her legs, what started as an ache became a hollowness that only he could fill.

Lost in the maelstrom of excitement, Davina hit the first peak, nerves wound tight as her fingers dug deep.

"More," he grunted, and continued the friction as she ratcheted into a shocking secondary spike of hunger.

His hands gripped her hips now, tugging her closer to the cataclysmic end.

"Micah," she screamed, aware that she was only seconds from orgasm, her body tighter than wire at breaking point.

"Now," he demanded, the final plunge brutal.

It wasn't just the fullness, the tight band of arms around her that pushed her senses to explode. Her chest full of emotions, wild and churning.

Starburst. Everything splintered, eyes unseeing, as the final crest breached. Crashing down, causing reality to spin away.

Together, they clung together. The instant of stillness that followed the wildness.

The sensation of his jetting soothing the edges as her mind whirled, and her chest heaved, seeking oxygen for starving lungs.

On wobbling legs, Micah stood and disengaged their bodies so she too could slide to the floor.

With a lurch, she dropped to sit on the end of the bed.

"I..." It didn't seem there could be any words to describe what they'd shared. "Wow."

He disappeared into the bathroom, returning only a moment or two later, minus condom but with a warm damp facecloth. "I thought you might appreciate some attention."

Micah placed a hand against her shoulder, and she lay back, intrigued at first, then touched as he gently wiped the dampness from between her legs.

"Thank you," she managed with a strangled voice, suddenly shy after the intimacies they'd shared.

Once he'd discarded the cloth, he settled down onto the bed beside her. She snuggled in, feeling the strength of the man as he carefully enfolded her in his embrace.

FOURTEEN

Micah studied the scene before him. Davina, lying on the divan in his workroom, artfully draped, her lush hair brushed back like a waterfall. Everything about this piece of work was right, and the inspiration was flowing.

The intimacy of the moment wasn't lost on him as he gazed at the woman lying on the chaise. "Can I see it yet?"

It wasn't the first time she'd enquired, but he wasn't ready to share the piece. It had to be finished and perfect.

He gave his attention back to the painting. "Soon, when it's done."

Her sigh echoed, and he couldn't control the snicker that rose. He lifted the chalk in his grip back to the canvas, considered where the next stroke should be as a peal broke the air.

"Oh Lord! Sorry, that's mine." Davina shifted so her breasts bobbed while she hunted beneath the seat where she'd stashed the robe and her phone and dragged it out. "Just a moment."

She grimaced as she inspected the caller ID. "It's my mother."

Setting down the utensil, he dropped to the stool as she answered.

"Hello, Mother."

"Davina. I've just rung your office, and they informed me you were taking some time off. I don't suppose that means you'll be coming to dinner with myself and my husband?" The waspish query had his brows drawing together in a painful frown.

"I'm uh, not sure. You said you were busy since returning from Bali and I know you like your space, so I planned nothing. Besides, why are you ringing? You usually only call at Christmas and when you're getting married or divorced."

"Davina Ann! What a terrible thing to say to your mother."

Now Davina straightened on the seat, tugging on the short robe and belting it tightly, her knuckles white against her already pale skin. "Because it's true. Look, tell me what you need me to do so I can sort it out."

"I just... Well, your father and that bitch he married are breeding again, and I realised I've not heard from you in a while..."

Davina's brows drew tight. These insignificant facts had never bothered her mother before, so why now? "What's going on?"

She heard the sniff and closed her eyes. Her mother always played the injured card just before she delivered the coup de grace, and obviously this was like every other time.

"Cassandra's daughter, Lilly, is engaged *and* pregnant. Sophie's son's wife is about to deliver her third grandchild and—"

So, her grandmotherly biological clock was ticking? That made no sense, given her mother was far too engaged with her love life and had stated many times that she was '*too young to become a grandpar-*

ent.' "Well, send them my congratulations. However, I'm busy right now, so—"

"Davina?" The tremulous sound speared right into her brain, the zing travelling fast and wide.

Davina rubbed at the now aching point between both eyes and wondered what else she would be requested to achieve. "*What?*"

"I was thinking maybe you should come by one night this week. Peter has the barbeque routine down pat."

Eyes crossed, Davina simply stared at the phone.

"Davina?"

"I'm ahh... I'm busy this week."

"Your office said you were on leave. Surely you could find some time to visit your mother and stepfather? It's not like you have a life. So, let me—"

"Mother, I'm kind of busy right now. Can I call you back?"

The sputter ricocheted through her. "Busy? You're on leave. You're not married and don't have kids. What could you *possibly* be doing that makes you so busy?" And there it was. The truth, according to her mother. The argument that cycled round again, every time. *I need you. You should be here for me. I'm the one who's hurting...* Would she never learn? To her mother, she was simply an unpaid assistant and free divorce lawyer on tap.

Blood pressure spiking, Davina gripped the phone. "Lots. Now I have to go. I'll ring you later." Hitting the end button wasn't anywhere near enough to ensure she washed off the frustration that welled. 'What could you *possibly* be doing?' Really?

Spinning on her heel, Davina faced the wall opposite as the sound of Micah's footsteps echoed. "Are you okay?"

"Yeah..." His fingers slid up and down her arms, as if he understood her inner turmoil.

It was just like her mother to ring, demand her presence, then throw a fit when Davina didn't kowtow immediately. But the wedding in Bali, the 'private ceremony for two' bullshit that constituted the final straw. She and her mother would never be close, and this was the final straw as far as Davina was concerned. "I'm a commodity to my mother. A contact that means free legal advice when this marriage goes bad."

"You don't mean that, Davina——"

Now she turned, movements sharp and uncoordinated. "I do. When she gets divorced—and she will once the initial glow of the lovey-dovey newly married statue wears off—I'll be called. My skills utilised for free while she wallows in the 'poor me' syndrome she excels at." It was impossible to blunt the sharpness of her tones, given the depth of her anger right now.

"Davina, you don't know——"

Davina knew exactly what he was going to say. *You don't know that.* But she did. This was part of a cycle she'd seen enacted over and again. "I do know, Micah! I've picked up the pieces! I've been the one to deal with her crying jags and her tantrums. I'm the one who helped pack bags and clear bathroom cabinets. I served the papers last time because she was 'too fragile'. Hell, I called the paramedics when she said she'd taken a handful of sleeping tablets and had to have her stomach pumped after stepfather number three. The one who wanted to get jiggy with his new wife's teenaged daughter at their reception!"

Anger spewed a lava that burned from the inside out. "I've had to be the responsible one my whole life. The one that picked up the pieces each time. *Me.*" The words just kept coming. The explosion of pain and hurt that had collected over the years. "I collected keys, arranged representation and sat through endless mediation meetings."

Sucking in an unsteady breath, legs wobbling, she stared at him, all the while knowing he couldn't understand the depths of her despair. "And I can't do this anymore."

She stalked from the studio, for the moment uncaring if he followed because she'd heard the way her voice cracked on the last word.

In the bedroom, her hands plucked at and removed the silky robe while she kept her mind carefully blank. She snatched clothing from the suitcase she'd brought and hauled them on to cover her nakedness.

He followed, footsteps echoing as the tattoo of pumping blood swirled in her brain. "I have to go. I need time and space." Davina couldn't stay. Her demons demanded nothing more than privacy so she could lick her wounds and her brain needed her to find some core of hard-won peace. If she didn't, she'd shatter like a wine glass at a Greek wedding.

She hurried for the bathroom, grabbing the toiletries pack and returned to shove it in her bag, which she zipped with a harsh jerk. "I'll call you."

He didn't follow, and right now, she didn't want him to. She needed time to prepare for what would come soon. God knew her mother would demand her pound of flesh for the outburst today.

Besides, it was time to let go of her own dream—the one that just emerged from a lifelong cocoon. The one that withered and died during one brief phone call.

CHAPTER

FIFTEEN

Micah allowed Davina to stew for three days. The fury that washed off her, swamping him, scorched him. He understood the anger, though he couldn't even attempt to come to terms with what caused it.

He spoke with his sister, his minister brother and even Fenella, his sister-in-law. Her parents were divorced, he theorized. Maybe she'd have pearls of wisdom.

"But how do I help her, Fenella?" He gripped the coffee cup in both hands.

Her gaze was soft and understanding. "To be honest, the breaking up of a family is hard on everyone involved. The kids even more so. Many feel it's their fault. I did for a long time. I had to learn and understand. It wasn't about me. But if her situation is as brutal as you've said, then she may need more than you and I can do. You say she picked up the pieces when her mother fell apart and that's so unfair. All you can do right now is give her time and space. A few days."

Instead, Micah used the time gainfully. During the day, he worked, the chalk sliding over the paper with quick and sure actions. Every move dictated by the passion that flared for his artwork. The

113

pieces each filling the void for the upcoming showing, while he avoided—as much as he could—wondering what Davina was doing. He'd give her the time she needed.

While that proved gratifying artistically, it didn't hold at bay the seed of doubt that crept into his mind about the situation with Davina. Not just the need to have her close, but losing a significant part of himself that he'd given her.

At night he meditated until he could grip onto some calm. It calmed his soul during his self-imposed exile. Nothing took away the concern or pain, though.

At night, when he lay in his empty bed, those seeds took root once more, so sleeping a series of hours spent tossing and turning, the scent of her on his pillows nearly driving him insane.

What if her mother's actions proved too much? What if Davina couldn't step away from the betrayal and hurt?

On the fourth day, he rose. Donned his clothes and put into action the plan he'd carefully crafted.

&

Davina tossed and turned after an uncertain night. She scooped up her running suit and sighed. She still had three days left of her break. The one she'd planned to spend with Micah.

Filling every day and looking for a meaningful use of her time was difficult to achieve. The first day she'd sat around, feeling sorry for herself. The second and third she'd cleared her wardrobe and pantry. But with those tasks complete, the day stretched ahead. What to do? Her eyes settled on the running shoes she'd left by the front door, and the idea took root. Today, she'd run. Adrenaline helped her to think.

It always helped to clear her mind. By the time she'd dressed, tied back her hair and grabbed the arm strap for her phone and keys —and some cash in case she needed it—her mind had firmed.

Letting herself out of the building took only a moment, and she'd settled on a path that took her past a small café, where she'd take a break, rehydrate before beginning the return home route.

Her feet found a rhythm steady, and Davina cleared her mind. Her mother posed a problem, as did Laura. Not that she didn't like Laura, she really didn't know her. The message left on her phone yesterday potentially changed the parameters of her life.

"Laura, what can I do for you?"

"I wanted to let you know we're moving home. Your father and I bought a house in Salling Heights."

Davina's stomach lurched. Salling Heights was only five minutes from her home. The haven she'd worked so hard to find. "Oh um... But what about his practice and the kids?"

Silence stretched. "I'm not totally sure about the school yet. I wanted to ask your opinion of the private school. You know, it might be nice that they have that in common with you."

Containing surprise and jealousy, she tightened her grip on the phone.

"Look, we don't have to talk about that now, though. I'm meeting some friends on Friday. Would you like to join us?"

Laura's earnestness had Davina backing off at a million miles an hour. "I've got plans for Friday." She really didn't, but this whole moving closer and getting-to-know-you thing wasn't what Davina needed right now. Besides, wasn't it like a decade or two too late?

She squinted in the sunlight, realizing she'd already come most of the way to the café, and slowed. Perspiration dripped as she left the park and crossed the road.

The handle to the café was cold as she slid it open and stepped inside.

Someone bumped her from behind in the busy store, and she turned. "Micah!"

He grinned, and the heat she'd been missing curled through her belly. "Oh, Davina! Sorry, I didn't see you."

His eyes crinkled, but shadows ringed them. "Are you okay?"

Without thinking, she reached up and touched his cheek. The smokiness she associated with his eyes stole her breath.

"Been working. How about you?"

His words rocked her back to reality. The fridge door open, and the coolness bathed her back. She turned, grabbed up the electrolyte rich drink and shut the door. "Good. Been running." *God, how inane does that sound?*

He smiled, and the punch of heat in her stomach quivered as it spread through her chilled body. "Rocking it too. Mind if I join you?"

"Oh, sure." She paid for the drink as the barista called his name and he surged to the counter to collect his coffee and they wandered to a quiet table in the corner.

"Busy today."

She settled in the seat. On an impulse she reached out her hand, "Yes. Look, Micah, I'm not sure what to do."

He leaned back in his seat. "What about?"

God, how hard was this? "Us."

Micah sighed. "I wasn't sure there was still an 'us'. After you left—"

"My mother has a way of doing this kind of thing. She rings. I react. It's a vicious circle." Twisting her fingers until they hurt, Davina hunted for a way to explain. "She's the sort that uses you. When she needs you, you're supposed to jump and ask how high on the way up. I wasn't what she wanted. But when my father left, she got me to herself. I learned early on to give her what she wanted because it made my life easier."

He frowned. "Parents don't let the kids do the work in the relationship."

"No, they aren't supposed to. Micah, would you come with me?" The words slipped out before she could haul them back.

"Where?"

Davina sighed. "She invited me to a barbecue at home. With the new husband. Will you come with me?"

"To your mother's house? Sure. When?"

She really hadn't meant to invite him, but he'd accepted, and the buffer would be more than welcome. "Tonight. At five." She closed off the seed of fury at herself. Not that she was using him, her brain reiterated. It just needed him and his presence to centre her.

"Want me to pick you up?"

She nodded. "Yes. Thanks."

They discussed the time, and she swallowed the last of her drink. "I have to get going."

Micah stood and followed her through the door, and her nerves jangled.

"Davina, you don't have to run away."

He spoke so tenderly that the wall around her heart, the one she'd carefully rebuilt over the last couple of days, exploded. When he reached out and took her hand, tears welled in her eyes, burning her. "Please."

"What do you want, Davina?"

And that was the problem. She wanted hearts and flowers. Romance. Love. Kids. The thing was, she wanted it with Micah, and that force of need terrified her.

She really should nip this in the bud. Tell him that this was it, but Davina couldn't bring herself to say the words.

He breached the distance between them, folding his arms around her so the sense of safety ricocheted through her brain.

Her fingers closed around his coat, holding him close as she burrowed in. "Micah..."

"I'm here for you. Whatever you need, Davina."

"Don't... Don't leave. Come home with me." The words tumbled out. Honest. Needy.

He tugged away, gaze searching her face with an intensity she'd never noticed. "Are you sure?"

She nodded. "Yes."

Micah released her hand and tugged her up the street until she saw his vehicle. The lights flashed as they neared, and he motioned her in.

It had only been a matter of days, and yet the minute she stepped into the car with him, it felt right. Like she'd come home. It gave her pause.

They sat in silence as he drove the vehicle to her place. He parked where he always had, and without a word, followed her to the door.

When it swung open, she turned and faced him before he entered. "Could you make a coffee? I'm going to take a quick shower and change." In a whirl, she left him there because the situation felt too intimate, and she needed a moment to regain herself.

The shower was warm, and the steam rose around her as she considered that she'd invited him back into her topsy-turvy world, but she refused to hide away. With a deep breath, Davina turned the handles, and the water ceased flowing. She towelled down and headed for the bedroom, finding comfortable lounge clothes.

Micah waited in the kitchen, his coffee steaming, and as she entered the room, he indicated to the one he'd made her.

"Let's talk."

His eyes narrowed. "About what?" They settled on the lounge chair, her perched inches from him. But the chasm felt like the Grand Canyon.

"I'm making a mess out of all of this." She muttered and rubbed her forehead. "I'm not a woman who can't decide or needs a man to make her whole or feel safe. I've been on my own for a long time and I like it that way. You're something else, though. You make me feel things I'd rather not. I need to question why I'm so afraid."

Instead of interrupting, Micah let her talk.

"I'm frightened that you'll mean too much to me and I'll do something, then you'll leave. That I won't live up to some ideal, Micah. I can't be like your mother or sister. I don't know how to be them."

"Good. Because I don't want them, Davina. Nothing needs to be decided today. There's no need to rush into a commitment. We can take this day by day. Whatever you need."

CHAPTER

SIXTEEN

The house they drove to was older, more weather beaten than the luxury apartments that had sprung up around it. "Some expensive real estate here."

"Mum refused to sell. She likes the postcode and the idea that she's in 'snobs' knob' more than she cares about the state of the house." Davina's tones betrayed her frustration.

"We can turn around and tell her we couldn't make it," Micah joked.

"She's already seen us. Notice the twitch of the lace curtain by the front door?"

He had and sighed. They climbed out and he trailed Davina to the door.

They didn't knock before it was flung open. "Oh... you've brought someone." Her mother appeared out of sorts, but he let it wash off him. He was here for Davina and that was all that counted.

"Mum, this is Micah. He's a friend and offered to bring me tonight. Where is..." she hunted through her memory for the name. "Where is Peter?"

Her mother giggled girlishly. "On the deck. He's grilling for me."

Footsteps echoed and a man in his fifties, with immaculate grey hair, appeared. "Oh, there you are, darling. And there's Davina. Hi." His smile was open, friendly. It thawed the tiniest chink of ice that froze her.

"Peter." She took his hand and shook it, then turned to Micah. "This is my friend Micah. He ummm... brought me over tonight."

The two men shook hands, and Peter indicated they should follow through the lounge to the outdoor area. "Maeve, why don't you go grab some glasses and wine and I'll keep Davina and Micah company?"

Her mother frowned, then nodded. "Yes. Of course."

The deck smelled of polish and sizzling meat, and she blinked. "The decks been oiled."

"Yes. I told your mother some maintenance would ensure the house remained in good shape. It's got great bones, just needs some love and care."

Davina's gaze narrowed. "You know the house is held in a trust, right?"

"Davina! I didn't raise you to be so rude. Peter is simply helping me look after the place!" Maeve's voice pealed over her and the urge to close her eyes and will herself far away flared.

"It's okay, Maeve. Yes, I know. I had your mother sign a prenup before we married, so her assets are protected if things don't go to plan."

Davina gasped as her mother thrust a glass of wine into her hands. "So...?"

"Just the same as I did for my assets. My daughter was horrified but as I told her at the wedding, it was her inheritance I was looking after."

"At the wedding?" Davina turned to her mother.

"Oh yes, Jane came with us as the witness," her mother chattered. "She's such a nice girl. Getting married soon and I can't wait."

Davina opened her mouth and closed it while Micah drew near, offering silent support. The anger inside her built, but she held on to Micah's hand. Hoping like hell she could stave it off. Peter appeared to be a nice man, and she didn't want to embarrass him or Micah with the outburst that would no doubt follow a loss of control.

"It was a shame you couldn't get away from work, Davina. It would have been so nice to have the four of us there. But I understand sometimes things come up. Your mother told me you're a solicitor?" His eyes settled on her, kind and understanding.

And the entire story my mother spun is a total bloody lie. For a moment, she wondered what he'd say if she told him?

"I work in family law. Mostly with low income, domestic violence and so on."

Peter frowned. "But isn't that hard?"

"Someone has to do it and it's something I'm good at."

He smiled and patted her hand. "So long as you enjoy it, my dear. I told Jane when I handed over control of the business that she had to love it, to make the time and effort worthwhile. Thankfully paint seems to run through her veins more than blood."

Dinner was a stilted affair. Maeve dropping hints about her friends with grandchildren on the way and weddings to arrange. Every comment a slice at Davina.

Micah filled in where he could until Maeve disappeared into the kitchen. "So, what do you do, Micah?"

"I'm a painter."

"Oh. Houses? High rise?"

On much more comfortable ground, Davina held his hand. "He's actually a pastellist. Micah McKay."

Peter's mouth dropped. "McKay? I've got one of your seascapes in my office. Well. My word. You've got a wonderful skill, almost magical in the way you bring your work to life."

Her mother appeared at the door. "I made your favourite, Peter, darling. Blueberry cheesecake."

By the end of dessert, Davina couldn't wait to escape. "Mother? Micah, and I need to go. Thank you for dinner. Peter, it was lovely." She didn't offer the usual 'I hope we meet again,' because somehow that would have been rude. Even if it was the truth from her perspective.

They left, and she closed her eyes once they were back in his car. "So, what did you think?"

Micah sighed. "I'm not sure I'm keen on your mother, but Peter seems nice."

A bubble of laughter rose. "I thought that too. I mean, Peter was trying, which is more than most of her men ever did. That he wanted her to keep her assets to herself too went a long way with me."

The drive home was quick, traffic having subsided, and they slipped into her home.

She tugged off her shoes, released her hair and dropped her bag onto the side table.

"Micah, you'll stay, won't you?"

"I will. But just to hold you. I think we both need time to work out how this relationship thing is going to work."

Saturday was a day of relaxation. Micah and Davina treated it no differently, waking later and trawling leisurely through the shops.

"I need groceries," Davina had declared, and he laughingly agreed, having seen the contents of her refrigerator, freezer and pantry.

Arriving home, they'd unloaded the bags and settled in with a movie.

"We should really meditate," she told him, her face aglow with, he guessed, embarrassment. "I've got some yoga pants and a bra top I could wear."

What a shame. He closed the door on the thought and smiled. "We could. I've got a bag in the car."

She laughed. "Pays to be prepared, huh?"

He'd ducked out that morning and dropped by his place, grabbing some necessary items in case she allowed him to stay a little longer. Not that he planned anything, but with Davina, he was always hopeful.

He'd just reached for his keys when Davina's phone pealed.

Instinct had him turning as she answered, her face wreathed in smiles that died away once she heard from whoever was on the other end of the line. "I'm on my way, Jane. Stay safe."

Her hands shook as she disconnected the call. "Can you take me to..." she gulped Micah's gut twisted.

"Anywhere, just tell me."

"The Gerrets Apartments on Hollington Street. Jane—one of my clients—was attacked by her ex-husband earlier today. She's... I need to get there."

"Come on, then." He ushered her out the door, grabbing her bag and keys as she sailed past him, a testament to her level of concern that she'd forgotten about them.

It was quick driving, but on arrival, police and ambulance officers milled at the front door.

"I'll need you to stay here, Micah."

Much as he wanted to be with her, though, he understood that she'd asked him to give her help where she most needed it, but also had a job to do. So, he gave a single nod. "If you need me, just call."

He waited by the car, eyes capturing the vision before him as she moved closer to the throng of officials. Whatever she'd said, there was initial consternation. Then an officer beckoned over, and she retreated within.

Micah waited. At thirty minutes, he moved slightly, so he leaned against the building. At the one-hour mark, she returned. Pale and drawn. "They're taking her downtown to the hospital. Her brother was transferred earlier. He's critical, but they had to question her first."

"How do you do this day-after-day, Davina?" The words slipped out and now she crumpled on herself. He cursed himself for a fool and dragged her close, across the centre console of the vehicle. "I'm a ham-handed twit, Davina. I shouldn't have said that."

Her shoulders quivered, but she shook her head. "No, you're right. I don't know how I do it. It's... There are so many things that go wrong in these cases. Jane's case, though, it spoke to me from the beginning. I guess I became too invested in her situation. She tried to get away from him, left with nothing except her purse, Micah. We applied for the restraining order and the judge refused it because he didn't think we had enough proof. Now she's lost the baby, her brother could die and all I can do is stand on the sidelines." Her words ended in a wet and garbled wail.

"But at what cost to you?"

"I know. I can't do this much longer. I want out, but I don't know what else I can do, Micah. Family law is all I've practiced for years."

His eyes burned in sympathy, because the cases had heaped upon her, the situation with her mother reinforcing the negative view of marriage. That she could even look at a man without either loathing or fear was a minor miracle.

"Do you want to go home, Davina?"

She shook her head. "I should go to the hospital."

"Why?"

Now Davina blinked, but the silence between them stretched.

"Would you normally?"

"No. No, I wouldn't, Micah. What I would normally do is start on the paperwork for an Order. I mean... I don't even know why he was released, but..."

"Office?"

This time when Davina shook her head, there was more force behind it. "No, home. I have everything I need there. I'll get the paperwork together, then lodge it online. Nothing can happen until I get a court date, but I can request a Temporary Protection Order until things can get rolling."

She slid on her seatbelt and satisfied she was safe; he started the car and headed for her home, the entire time considering what she'd said. He wouldn't press her for details, understanding the confidentiality of the situation, but he could and would offer her moral support.

CHAPTER

SEVENTEEN

O n Sunday, Micah helped Davina with the washing. She was quiet, and he wondered what was going through her mind. By eleven, he was urging her out the door. "Family lunch date," and she smiled wanly, as if her mind were a million miles away.

Once they returned to her apartment, she disappeared into her office, reappearing three hours later, tired but with the first natural smile she'd shared all day.

"I've extended my leave. I need time to think and to be honest, now that I have a PA, this is the best time."

"Best time for extending your break?"

She shook her head. "No. Jane's case hit me harder than any other I've been involved with. I think it's time I investigate other options and choices. I mean, I like the people I work with. It's a great office mostly, but the work is getting to me. The last week, I've been able to concentrate on other things and it showed me I don't want to continue down this path."

"Okay, so what do you want?"

"I don't know work wise, but I want whatever it is you're cooking." She sniffed the air, and he smiled.

"It's not finished, so you're just in time to help me out."

She laughed again and his own mood lightened. "What do you need me to do?"

Micah passed her a spoon and directed her to the stove top. "Stir that while I get started over here."

They chatted while he washed and tore lettuce, chopped the soft white fetta and prepared the other vegetables he planned to toss into the salad.

Once the aroma wafted through the room, he came over, lifted the lid on a saucepan, and tossed in spaghetti.

"Bolognese from scratch?"

"Yup. My favourite version of it, anyway. I add a few extras and since it's an easy meal, I can impress the important women in my life."

She gifted him a mock leer. "How many girls?"

"Just you and my sister. Oh, and sister-in-law of course!"

"Just as well you said that, otherwise I think Fenella would be really put out." Davina wagged her finger at him.

"Davina, would you come back to my place tomorrow? I need to complete some pieces and prepare for the showing." He waited, unsure if she'd agree.

"I need some time to do a little shopping, so how about I head over once I'm done. I have some things I need to attend to." Her voice dropped to a subdued level again, and he wondered if she planned on catching up with Jane.

"Would you like me to come with you?"

Davina shook her head, hair flying. "No. Honestly, I just need some time."

He backed off, refusing to push her for any commitment she wasn't ready to give. "Sure. You know where the studio is, just come through when you get there, then."

He took a quick look into the saucepan, tested the spaghetti and declared it 'al dente' and started serving.

C hances were, Micah had already worked out what she planned, Davina thought as she entered the hospital wing. Seeing Jane was simply the first step in what she needed to do, having considered long and hard the day before how she'd felt about her work. It had taken Micah's questioning on Saturday night to make her aware that she'd given so much of herself to her job, that there was little left for her or a life. Micah made her see that.

It was time to make a change.

Not that she planned to abandon any other clients—far from it— but she'd be informing her boss that Jane's case was the last she'd take on and see through to the end. She intended to resign. A plan of action formed in her mind.

She'd take on a bridging course, though deciding which branch of law she'd move to still eluded her. "I have time."

The ding of the elevator reaching its floor dragged her from her introspection and she stepped into the hallway. At the nurses' desk she stopped and requested the room Jane's brother was in and moved swiftly, knocking and entering at Jane's "come in."

"Hi Jane. How's Edward coming along?"

The woman gave her a tremulous smile. "He regained consciousness overnight, and the doctors said he'll pull through. They're moving him onto a ward later today."

"That's splendid news." She reached out and squeezed the woman's shoulder. "I wanted to see how you were both getting on, but I've requested a Temporary Protection Order, so that's a huge step forward. Can you sign some paperwork for me?"

The woman nodded and accepted the papers. "I just want to move on, Davina. I don't want to live my life hiding from Danny."

She flicked through the pages, found the place where she had to sign, then pushed it back to Davina.

She took a moment to stash them in her bag. "I won't promise what I can't do, but I'll do my best for you Jane."

The woman nodded, and for a moment, they sat in silence.

"Have you spoken to anyone? Therapists?"

Jane's glance, rolling her eyes, spoke volumes. "They're fine with the physical stuff, but the one I saw yesterday didn't have a clue about DV, so I'm not sure they're going to be more than a little stuck for help. But Edward and I are going to see the DV counsellors once we're out of here."

"Good." Now Davina's voice sounded rusty.

Jane's gaze narrowed. "Are you okay?"

Unbidden, tears threatened, burning her eyeballs. "Yes, and no. Jane, I wanted to tell you I'll be resigning from my job."

The woman's face shuttered. "I see. Who will take over the case?"

Shaking her head and reaching out with a trembling hand, Davina cursed her delivery. "No. You're the last case I'll see through to the end. I'm going to stay with you, Jane. I won't abandon you to someone else."

As Jane's gaze narrowed, Davina sighed. "Look, I said that wrong. What I meant was I've decided once I see your case through, I plan to move to another sector of law. I got invested in your case. I feel for you Jane, and I intend to see you get what you deserve, but I've realized I need a life away from what I do now."

The woman sat there, watching her. "So, what will you do?"

Now Davina sighed. "That I don't know yet."

The knock on the door signalled the arrival of the doctor and Davina excused herself, assuring Jane she'd be in touch soon.

She made her way slowly to the exit and turned left, wandering to the taxi rank, gave directions to her office and waited in silence as they travelled the distance. Once there, she paid off the driver and headed inside to hand to documents to Mel, who assured her she'd attend to them.

It was only when Davina walked back out the office door that she drew a deep breath. Now she accepted the awareness that she'd already begun distancing herself from her role. Davina was more than ready to do something about the way her job had dominated her life. "No more," she muttered and crossed the road to the mall opposite.

The seed of rebellion urged her to shop, and Davina wandered the stores, looking for a wardrobe that included new underwear. It occurred to her, most of her wardrobe was chosen for the appropriateness of her work and now that she'd made the break, she'd need more leisurely clothes, comfortable and without the harsh lines of her daily work garments.

She carried a pile of bags as she headed for the refreshment area and caught sight of Laura, laughing with friends.

Too late to turn away, Laura caught sight and called her over. Davina sighed. *No help for it.*

She settled at the table of the small eatery and a waitress hovered. "Small cappuccino thanks."

"Davina, it's great to see you." Indeed, Laura grinned and there was only a friendliness in her face, but it still ratcheted up her discomfort.

"Yes. Timing, wasn't it?" She answered. "You've been shopping?"

"What? Oh, yes. Your father and I are trying to decide how to dress the nursery. Given this is likely my last chance to indulge in baby shopping, and it's a new house, I felt I should try."

Make an effort. Great, just so long as they expect nothing else from me, Davina thought sourly.

The others at the table rose and made their goodbyes and Davina felt a pang of guilt as the others left. "I'm sorry Laura, I didn't mean to interrupt."

Laura patted her hand. "Not at all. They joined me for a cup of coffee while I drink my decaf tea." She made a moue of distaste and Davina couldn't help the amusement that bubbled inside her.

"Okay."

The waiter returned with her coffee, and for a moment, she and Laura sipped in silence. "Actually, it's fortuitous timing, Davina. Your father and I were planning on inviting you to lunch. It's Austin's birthday, and we wanted you to join us."

Davina's gut quivered. "Oh…"

"Look, I know things aren't easy between you and your father, but we'd love for you to join us. Saturday at Bayside?"

"I might be joined by… a friend." Were you even supposed to say lover to your stepmother?

"Of course, you can. He's…?" Laura peered at her, questions in her gaze.

"Micah's a… He's a painter."

"Good looking?" she queried, and Davina blinked, unbalanced by the girl-friend way Laura was talking. The only other time she'd met her had been at their wedding, and that had been difficult. Stilted even. The only thing she'd kept from all her father's partnerships was the odd photo. Including one of Laura, her father, and the kids she'd put to one side with her mother's photo.

For the first time, Davina wondered if the distance she'd kept between them had hurt more than helped. Would she like Laura if she got to know her? She'd never even met these half siblings, unlike her half-brothers Dave and Josh. Dave, the nearest her age, hadn't kept in touch, deciding that they had nothing in common and Josh… *He'd be about fifteen now.*

Davina drained her drink and rose. "I need to get on."

Laura's brow knotted. "You're not at work? You're not sick, are you?"

"What? Oh! No. I'm taking some time off. I've got some things I need to attend to so I wanted a rational mind to think about what happens next." She moved with speed, now gathering up her bags. "I'll see you Saturday." On those hasty words she beat a retreat.

Micah finished the last stroke and stood back, wondering what Davina would say when she saw this piece. Even as he considered it, tapping footsteps hurried in his direction and he whipped around as his agent whirled into the room.

"How's my favourite client going today? Achieving..." Her voice died away and the need to growl rose in his throat.

"No."

"Micah, it's amazing." The breathlessness of her voice told him all he needed to know. "It's going to be a hell of a headliner at the showing."

He turned the easel around, feeling that her peering at the work was an invasion of his privacy. He'd never felt this with Karen, but then, this piece was *intimate*. Only for him and Davina.

"No. It's not going into the showing, Karen. This one is not for public display, yeah?"

She frowned. "But there's such depth and..." Her gaze sharpened. Lips twitching. A grin emerged and his gut clenched, a premonition of what was about to come hammering into him. "You've fallen for her, haven't you? That's why you won't let me show it off. Well, lucky her and bad luck for all the other women in the world. But that doesn't fix the issue of a headliner."

"I have something else in mind," he growled, and she raised her eyebrow.

"And?"

He stomped to a canvas he'd stashed earlier in the day for her to see. "Here."

It was a moonscape, shades of onyx and deep sapphire, lit with a bright yellow/white moon and trees that almost leaped off the canvas. Each move to the side appeared to affect them like a breeze.

"It's marvellous. Stunning. Not as good as the portrait, but your work has stepped up another level," she enthused, eyes glowing.

"Yeah, well, now you know. So, I've got twenty as per request."

Karen gave a sigh. "It's such a small gallery, showing only highly sought-after pieces and artists. If you have anything to bring home when the showing is over, I'd be surprised. You'll need to get to work quickly. I've had a request from a gallery in London and another in New York for your works."

"Yep. Sure." His attention settled somewhere over her shoulder and Karen blinked.

"Are you listening Micah?" Of course, he wasn't. Davina stood in the doorway, smiling at him.

"Karen, isn't it?" Davina entered quietly and Karen whirled around.

"Yes, and there you are Davina. Well, whatever you've done to Micah, keep it up. His work is amazing."

Karen scooped up her capacious black bag. "I'm going. Micah, I'll need an inventory from you by the end of the week and we'll need to arrange for the framing." She sashayed from the studio, Davina's eyes following her.

"She's a force to be reckoned with."

He laughed. "True, but she's not the one for me. That's you."

Davina allowed her mouth to tick into a small smile, with just an upturn of the corner of her lips. "You amaze me. But anyway, I uh, would you like to come to a family lunch with my…? My father and his wife, Laura, invited us."

"Sure. Where and when?" he asked, wiping his hands clear of the chalk dust, then leaning in for a soft drugging kiss.

Davina pulled back. "Go shower first and I'll kiss you properly."

His laugh echoed as he grabbed her hand and towed her behind him. "Only if you agree to wash my back."

CHAPTER

EIGHTEEN

Davina tugged at the dress she wore for maybe the millionth time. "You're sure this is okay?"

Micah rolled his eyes and turned off the car. "You look fantastic. Good enough to eat, which I fully intend to when we get back."

Davina coughed, spluttered, then laughed. "Maybe you should ask first. You know, like it says in the manuals?" The banter soothed her ragged nerves as they climbed out of the car.

"True. That's the way to enlightenment." Micah grabbed her hand and together they headed into the restaurant. They gave the party name at the stand and were quickly pointed to the back of the room, where Laura and her father sat.

The children conspicuous by their absence and Davina frowned.

"Something wrong," Micah asked.

Biting her lip, Davina answered, "I thought it was a family lunch." Her head whirled with the range of reasons this may be, though she moved toward the table.

Laura rose, as did her father. The air between them strained.

"Thanks for coming, Davina," her father muttered, and Laura looked close to tears.

"What's wrong?" Micah's voice slid between the couples, a barrier and a question.

"The children didn't want to come, so we arranged a babysitter. The move has unsettled them, but I wanted today to be about family," Laura spoke quietly, and the gaze she shot at her older husband was pleading.

It felt intimate to Davina's way of thinking. Something she really wasn't sure she was ready to comprehend.

They settled in their seats; the waiter doing the rounds asking what they'd like to drink, and Davina felt deep surprise at the way her father took Laura's hand, ordering two tonic waters for them, while she and Micah settled on a glass of white wine.

"So, Davina. Did you accomplish everything you planned to do the other day?" Laura's voice broke through the uncomfortable air.

"Oh, well, yes and no." How did she explain to her stepmother she had almost no experience with family life? It was clear his wife wanted to change the situation, but where did Davina fit into the picture? Then she also needed to add that into the mix, that she was about to embark on a career change. And Micah.

Micah rubbed soothing circles on her back, showing he was aware of her concerns. "She's thinking of making some changes in her life," he said, and all eyes settled on Micah.

Davina felt both grateful and nervous about the change of tactics. Especially when her father's gaze narrowed.

"And I don't know you."

"I'm Micah McKay. Thirty-six and a Pastellist. I'm about to embark on a showing at the Radcliffe Gallery and my agent has been contacted by galleries overseas." Micah's movements didn't change, and she understood it was because he was comfortable, assured in who he was and what he did.

"You're a painter?" Her father leaned closer. "Making money?"

Micah laughed while Davina cringed.

"I do pretty well for myself, own my own home in Hatherington, with a view of Night Rocks from the porch. My car is new, and I have a reasonable amount of cash in my account."

"Micah!" Davina gasped, "Micah!" just as Laura did, similar to her father.

Micah laughed and her father grunted. "Just wanted to know a little about him."

Davina shot a look of anger at her father. "I'm not sure you're deserving of the information. You—"

"Davina, wait." Micah murmured in her ear, and she stilled, turning just enough to see his face and the intensity of the gaze.

"I know you feel I left you all those years ago, Davina. I've wanted to talk to you for a long time, but you've always been defensive. Unwilling to hear."

The drinks finally arrived, and Davina took a sip, wondering how she could stem from this conversation.

"Look. I get that now you're back in town. It feels uncomfortable having me living in the same area and not 'close', but I'm all grown up. I don't need a Daddy. I also don't want to be the answer to your wounded pride when you look back." She made to rise, hurt scalding deep inside.

"I didn't want to leave. I started proceedings to take you with me, but my lawyer said I'd never get custody, but I rang every day for months. Your mother said you didn't want to talk to me."

Like the air sucked out of a balloon, Davina dropped, deflated, into her seat. "No."

Micah's arm wound around her, the supportive anchor in a sea of hurt and regret. *Could mum have done this to me?* The answer was yes, she could. But if she had...

"So, why did you wait so long? Why didn't you fight for me?"

Her father shook his head, his eyes glittering with moisture. "You were a girl, and my life was filled with my work. Surgeons aren't home much, so how could I parent you properly? Then I remarried. Dave was born, and you were older. I didn't know how to reconnect.

Time passed, Davina. Time that I should have spent with you. Every year I sent presents for Christmas and birthdays, but I kept my distance, waiting for you to come to me. It was only after Laura and I married I decided to try again."

Laura reached out. Her hand grasping Davina's cold skin. "He regrets the years, Davina. Please. We want to know you. To be part of your life."

"I can't—"

Words failed and once more Micah came to the rescue. "Maybe enough has been said for today. Why don't we order and just enjoy lunch together?"

Davina ordered, ate, but her mind was engaged in thinking over actions, words. What had gone before.

The years she'd spent unwanted and merely an appendage to parents too self-involved to care for her.

The air at the table was thick, and when Davina and Micah made to leave, Laura pressed an envelope into her hand. "You don't have to come, but I'd appreciate your presence."

Still far too upset to think further, Davina shoved the envelope into her bag and together she and Micah left the restaurant in silence.

CHAPTER

NINETEEN

Micah thought over what Laura and Ashton—Davina's father—said. He'd wanted to keep in contact. The thing was, Ashton hadn't, and Davina had suffered. Even now, face averted from him, as she struggled with emotions that ravaged her. Her shoulders shaking, hands tightly clenched.

What to do? His mind churned. They were lovers, emotionally engaged, but enough for him to say anything that would mean enough? That he didn't know.

They arrived home, and she remained quiet. Subdued.

His chest ached as pain radiated from the woman beside him.

It grew, blooming until he could stand it no longer. He rose, reached out a hand, and pulled her with him to his bedroom. Pleasure. He'd give her that if nothing else. From the draw at the base of the bed, he tugged out a large bath sheet and flicked it onto the bed, all the while Davina watched him.

"Lie down but take off your clothes."

Her eyes asked the question.

Micah cupped her face. "For you. Tonight, the pleasure is yours, Davina. Let me care for you as no one else has or can."

She reached her hands up, and started stripping while he moved around the room, matches setting alight candles. The heady fragrances of lavender and ginger filling his senses. In the tiny bathroom, he found the rose scented massage oil he'd bought, then discarded it for lemongrass, the bottles clinking.

When he re-entered the room, she'd already chosen music, and it played softly in the flickering light.

Micah divested himself of clothing, wishing they'd both bathed, but this had been a spur-of-the-moment decision and he would not kill the mood with a demand.

Davina had mounded the pillows, and she lay on her stomach, eyes closed.

"Comfortable?"

"Yes." It was the first word she'd spoken in over an hour, and he wondered if it meant she'd relaxed her guard a little.

It gave him heart, and he climbed onto the bed, stationed himself at her feet and looked at the miles of bare skin. "I'm going to touch you, Davina."

"Mmm…" she responded.

He twisted the cap, poured the oil into his cupped hand and set the bottle on the table beside the bed, while the liquid in his palm warmed.

With slow moves, he set it to the skin of her calf and made careful moves up and down, determined to only serve her needs. Those of his body, the throb of arousal he ignored. Her skin shone in the light, flickering, and the scents heightened his awareness as muscles quivered and jumped beneath his ministrations. Over her derriere, and here he slid his fingers a little longer than normal, enjoying the way she responded to his touch.

Reaching her shoulders, he felt the tension and fine tremors that wracked her.

"Would you turn over for me, Davina?"

He heard the throatiness of his request and heard the sigh of her agreement as she moved.

His loins tightened further, the ache in his groin intense as her eyelids, half mast, couldn't disguise her arousal. The jut of nipples, cherry pink and the way she couldn't quite remain still.

"Micah?" The word she spoke, husky with sensual hunger.

"No. Not yet. Pleasure." It took everything to continue cupping the oil again and applying it. He started with her feet, and she moaned. He moved the motions to her legs, and she shifted, widening them so he could access her inner thigh. His hands glanced at the folds that hid the intimate skin, breath stolen as she shifted, the hairs brushing over his knuckles.

Her belly quaked when he reached it and even before he approached where chest became breasts, sweat poured down his back.

"Come to me, Micah."

Her lips opened and heaven help him, he couldn't resist the siren call of her voice. Leaning in was the only option, and he gave himself over to sharing the pleasure he'd so badly wanted her to enjoy.

Their lips clung. Mated. Soft, drugging kisses that pulled him further into her sensual web.

The gentle touch of her, tugging him closer so their bodies slid together, every move erotic and subtly fragrant, the oil on her skin heating further.

Now he wrapped himself around her, arms holding her close while he felt the hammering measure of her heartbeat.

Fingers speared through hair as tongues clashed and danced, his feet pushing her legs apart.

Chest straining, he pulled away. "I wanted you to feel cared for, Davina. Not taken from."

Her smile, intimate and knowing, captured him, nearly breaking his heart. "I know. But I want this with you, Micah."

Davina scooted down the bed, settled herself with her gaze fully on him. "Come inside me, Micah. Share your body with mine."

His hand slid down her length, over skin that undulated beneath his glancing touch, and slid between her legs. "Like this?"

Her throat moved; her eyes closed. "Not. More. You. All of you."

He laughed, strained though it was. "More?"

Now he positioned himself, the head of his cock nudging at her. "Like this?"

"Oh, yes." The whisper called and drugged him, urged him as he nudged his hips, watching as the tip slid within her.

A gentle movement, only a slight arching, but he slid all the way. Home.

"I love you, Davina." The words burst from him as his hands found grip on her hips and the dance, aeons old, began.

He thrust, and she crooned. Her hands curled into the bedding, as if she sought something to ground her.

The heat inside him blooming. Warmth spreading and the need, so all-consuming, welled. A dam ready to overflow, and now the hunger gnawed at him, while every move they made fed the ravening beast that lived inside of him.

"Mine," he growled.

"All yours," Davina agreed, the cry thin as the sensation of her orgasm milked him.

"Micah!" This time she arched off the bed, eyes open yet blind in the throes of her passion and he let go, released himself with a last move. Jetted deeply inside her as his chest bellowed.

He strained.

Muscles corded and fingers bit deep.

Time had no meaning, only the touch of Davina.

Of love.

Time passed, and his body calmed. Now he moved slowly, languor giving his limbs a soft feeling.

Sated, Micah rolled to the side, taking her with him, keeping her close. Against his heart, where she belonged.

"Did you mean it?" Her voice sounded thready, as if the emotions were too much for her to hold on to.

"Yes, Davina." In his mind, there was no question. She completed him.

She clutched at him. "Don't leave me. Don't let me go," the demand echoed through him.

"Never."

❧

Davina's fingers tapped on the keyboard of the computer. Her mind whirled with the words Micah had spoken the night before. *I want to believe him.*

So much in her life had changed in the last few months and she felt at sea. Confused.

The whole idea of love scared her. She wanted, desperately, to take his words at face value. Nothing about her life was what she'd expected or planned for. She'd been so sure that being alone and protecting her heart was the only answer. Then there was work. It no longer fulfilled her instead, it had beaten her down. Reinforced what she'd 'known' so she'd been isolated. Now she wanted more.

Biting her lip, Davina refocused on the screen before her. So many kinds of law. Criminal law didn't appeal. The negative emotions she'd experienced with family law reinforcing she wanted —needed—something that would fill the emptiness that she now carried inside her.

But what did that leave? Commercial law would allow her to go home at night, but did it give her the satisfaction she sought? Something else came into view and she tapped a key, opening a new screen.

Her phone buzzed and without thought, Davina answered, "Hello?"

"Davina Ann. I tried ringing earlier, but you didn't answer." *Mother.*

"Sorry, I got caught up." And she had. With Micah. The memory brought a smile to her lips. She'd meant to ring back, but he'd caught her sneaking into the shower and one thing led to another.

"Well, I was talking to Sandra Freeson today. She said she'd seen something odd and couldn't wait to tell me all about it. Her daughter, Alison, is married to that nice doctor James McMurtry, and they were at lunch yesterday." Same as ever. Davina scanned the screen, looking at the information presented before her, half listening to her mother's chatter.

It wasn't unusual for her to need to 'share' the gossip from her group of friends and acquaintances with her. Not that Davina had any clue why these snippets were even marginally important.

"Anyway, they went to that new restaurant, Bayside?"

Now her attention swung totally to her mother, and confusion gave way to something that felt suspiciously like a mixture of guilt and horror.

"Uhhh...."

"Imagine when Sandra says she saw you there with that painter fellow. Meeting another couple. An older couple." The snarl in Maeve's voice turning strident. "I thought to myself, well, they've gone to meet his parents without me. That was bad enough, until she told me—here's the thing, Davina Ann—she told me who you lunched with."

"Mother—"

"Now, I can't imagine why you've gone behind my back to have lunch with that snake and his bitch..."

Davina's ire rose. "Mother! This is not about you. Whether I meet with Father or not, you're divorced and have been for a very long time, and as an adult, I don't believe it's any of your business. I don't discuss him with you, nor do I expect—"

"Enough!" her mother bellowed and the fury in Davina's breast warred with horror at the level of spite her mother spewed.

Anger burned. "Did you stop him from seeing me?" The words slid out, and she winced at the neediness in the query.

"Of course, I did! What else would you expect me to do when he walked out that day?"

For a moment shock coursed through Davina. "You told me lies. You said he never wanted to know me."

"What difference does it make? He wasn't there. Besides—"

"Don't you dare!" Davina's fingers gripped the phone and Micah came dashing into the lounge where she'd been working. She didn't look at him, because right now, she had to push away the scouring fury. *Everything he'd said was true...*

"Davina Ann. I'm your mother and—"

"No." Her voice shook with emotion, while her chest felt set to explode. "I will not let you do this to me." Tears welled, and she dashed them away. "This is how it will be from now on, Mother. If I meet with my father and Laura, it's none of your business. I do not interfere in your entanglements, romantic or otherwise. You either respect my choices or I'll have nothing more to do with you." The words weren't idle threats, either. She had reached the end of her limit of tolerance. This final infraction pushing her beyond anything she'd endured previously. "I'm going to hang up now, Mother. I'll talk with you later, when I'm feeling more settled." Without another word, she depressed the key, then laid down the phone.

Only now did she look up at Micah, who waited in the doorway.

"Your mother?"

Davina nodded, her eyes burning with unshed tears. "Yes. I really don't want to talk about it right now, but I'd appreciate a cup of tea."

On a hiccup, Davina rose and tottered in his direction, then sighed when he pulled her into his arms. "My family is pretty dysfunctional," she said into his chest.

He laughed, the rumble settling her frustration and anger as nothing else every had. "Maybe they are, but I don't care, Davina. You and me? We can make our future whatever we want it to be."

Even as she released the steel holding her spine rigid, she wondered, *do I even know how to?*

TWENTY

Micah watched as Davina shuffled through her bag, looking for her purse. "It's in here somewhere."

"I can pay for it," he rasped, and she laughed.

"No. It's my treat. I said I'd cook dinner and I will." The grocery cart was filled with fruit, vegetables, and meat, and he wondered what she planned. "Ah ha!" She whipped it out with an envelope adhered to the side. "Oh, what's this?"

He leaned in. "Was it the thing Laura gave you at Bayside?"

When she bit her lip, the curl of hunger in his belly nudged at him, reminding him that the interest was never far away.

"I don't know."

The people behind cleared their throats, so they quickly paid for the food and left the store, the envelope safely stashed in her handbag. Once they'd climbed into the car, the groceries on the backseat, Micah turned to Davina.

"Should you open it?" This time, the bite of her lip tugged at him with concern. He understood she felt that dealing with her family was her responsibility, but Micah couldn't help wondering if she realized she no longer had to do it alone.

"I should." Her fingers dipped into her bag and drew out the envelope. They shook as she broke the seal. A tiny piece of paper slipped out.

He gave her a second, only to be rewarded with an "Oh God!"

Protective instincts on high alert, he scanned her face, which crumpled. "They want us to join them for a lunch next Sunday. At their house."

"And?"

"It's a family lunch for Carrie's birthday. She's turning six." She rubbed her aching brow. "I didn't go to Austin's last month."

He blinked. "You don't want to go?"

"I do, I think. My mother poisoned me, refused my father access. Then, when I was older, I shut him out every time he tried to make contact. I haven't even met Carrie or Austin, but they want me to join them at her birthday party." Tears dribbled down her face. "I missed out on so much, Micah."

Now he gathered her close, his eyes closing with thankfulness that the message was positive. "Families forgive, Davina. That's what the do best. They forgive. They try again."

"I didn't know. But now... Micah?"

"Yeah?"

"I..." she trembled in his embrace. "I love you, Micah."

His heart thudded, and he was sure it was audible. Blood whooshed and roared while exultation crashed over him. *She loves me.*

She lifted her teary eyes to his, her gaze earnest. "I've never said that before, because I was never looking for anything close to what I feel for you. I'm a coward, Micah. With you though, it's just there."

He raised a hand to cup her cheek. "Thank you," he rasped. The need to say more clawed at him, but not now. Not here. "We should get some wine," he suggested, and she pulled away with a wet laugh.

"Wine?"

"To celebrate, my love." He started the car as satisfaction filled his chest. She loved him. The trip home was swift once they'd chosen a bottle of champagne and He herded her into the kitchen, his mind whirling with ideas.

"Come with me," he requested, taking her hand and leading her into the studio.

She followed him, silent and probably wondering what he was doing.

The easel was still turned away and nerves ran through him. What if she didn't like it?

There was only one way to tell, so he cleared his throat, and picked it up, careful to obscure the view until he was ready to stand back.

Her gasp filled the air. "That's me," wonder filled her voice. Her hands shook, tears glistened in her eyes.

"This is the woman I see."

There she lay, the blue velvet of the chaise a foil for her perfect skin, hair tumbling down like a waterfall over her shoulder. The look in her eye soft and caring.

"That's me, but not me. I mean, I don't look like that. Not really."

He grasped Davina's shoulders, desperate to have her understand. "*It is you*. The softness not just of your skin, but the woman below the surface. The empathy you show your clients, who you've given everything for. The beauty that radiates from inside you." Davina gaped at him, but the words kept tumbling out. "The you, which you've hidden away, and have only let me see. You're the woman I love, Davina. But this gift," he motioned to the work before them, "this is for you."

"Micah, what will we do with it?"

Now he grinned. "I'm going to have it framed, then hung in our bedroom. For us, you and I only."

When she gasped, he winked. "I have no intentions of sharing it with anyone else. Ever."

Drawing her close, he kissed her hand.

Her fingers slid over his cheek to cup the back of his head and draw him to her. The kiss started slow and soft, a gentle mating of lips.

Without thought he deepened it, his arms winding around her, dragging Davina close and fitting her form against his.

When his lips found the pulsing vein at her neck, she moaned her desire, its twin burning hotly within him. It took every ounce of willpower to drag himself away from her, and they were both left breathing heavily. "We should attend to dinner."

Her blank gaze took a moment to clear, and she blinked. "Dinner. Yes."

The car pulled up beside the large white house. Boxy, but with large panes of glass gazing out into the bay. "Wow."

Micah turned off the engine. "Ready?"

"Yeah."

They climbed out of the car and Davina darted to the back, gathering up the brightly wrapped package from the back seat. "I hope she likes it."

She had little knowledge of young girls and without even knowing her half-sister choosing the present had been difficult. In the end, she'd talked to Micah's sister-in-law, Fenella, who had given her some suggestions.

Trepidation filled her knees, wobbling as she made her way to the gate. Micah beat her, pressed the buzzer on the gate.

"You're here! Great, I'll let you in," called Laura and when Davina looked up, it was to see her stepmother standing on the veranda, one hand on her distended belly, the other on the small of her back.

A buzz echoed, and the gate blocking their way opened. Before they'd even reached the door, her father was there waiting. A half smile on his face, some tension lines she'd previously noted before, smoothed away.

He didn't reach to hug her the way she'd seen other fathers do, but the welcome in his gaze settled some nerves which fluttered inside her belly.

"Davina and Micah. We're pleased you could join us." He ushered her up the stairs as the noise and hustle of two young children filled the air.

One whipped by her, and she turned side-on to let them pass and down the steps.

"Austin," called her father, and the little boy stopped.

"What?"

"Come back upstairs, I want you to meet some people."

"Who?" the little boy queried, then blinked up at her. "Are you my sister?"

A lump settled in her throat, and she glanced at Micah, who gave her a smile.

"Yeah. I'm Davina."

"Hi," he answered, then tore past her up the steps.

It took a moment for her to clear her mind, then she followed him up. Laura waited at the top of the steps, and once they'd all entered the sizeable room, she shut the gate behind them. "Keeps everyone safe," she explained, then gave Davina a hug. "Welcome home."

Laura moved on, but Davina stayed where she was over-whelmed. *Home.* It wasn't like any home she'd ever known, yet even with the expensive furnishings and artwork on the wall, it felt just like that.

Ashton headed down the hall and returned with a young girl in a pink princess dress in his arms. "Come say hello to your sister, Davina, Carrie."

The little girl smiled. "Is that for me?" and reached out her arms.

Unsure what to do, Davina handed over the parcel. "Happy birth-day, Carrie."

With a squeal, the girl settled on the floor and tore into the wrap-per. When she'd uncovered the item within, she screamed, "I wanted one of these!"

Laura laughed, and Ashton bent down. "Come say thank you, Carrie."

The girl launched herself one-armed to her, the large unicorn plush toy firmly entrenched in her other arm. "Thank you, Davina."

From the outside came a teen. Her half-brother Josh. She knew him slightly, and he waved. "Hi Davina."

Now she turned to her father. "Dave?"

"Couldn't get away. He's been posted overseas with the bank and leaves in three weeks, but he wanted to come. There's so much to do before he goes, such as packing up his house and his girlfriend Lisa is going with him. There's her family to catch up with. He's going to try and get up in a week or so."

"Oh." She didn't know about this Lisa, and the fact she knew so little about her family made it hard to offer anything useful.

"Come on through," said Laura as she ushered the group to the veranda set up with a long table decorated in pink and purple.

It was an enjoyable lunch, if strange. The turkey and vegetables incongruous in the summery heat, but Laura assured her they were Carrie's favourites, so she'd indulged the child.

"Can I help?" she offered at one point, only to be hushed.

"No. Your father is in charge of birthday meals. I simply do the organisation and shopping," Laura told her.

With the meal finished, Josh stood. "I have to go home. Mum's coming to get me. She and her friend are taking me to the Sea Escapades." Once he'd left, Austin and Carrie retreated to their rooms, Austin for a nap and Carrie to play with Stella, her new unicorn. Micah assisted her father, clearing the table while Laura and Davina sipped on cooling drinks.

When Micah and her father settled themselves back in the seats at the table, Davina knew what she needed to do.

"Father, I spoke to Mother. She told me what she did." The words hung in the air, and he sighed.

"I should have fought for you, Davina, but I honestly thought it was the right thing to do. I hoped there'd be time, when you got older, for you to accept that I'd tried to make the right choices."

Micah reached for her hand and squeezed.

"I was young when we married. Still in school, and she was the girl everyone wanted to be seen with. When we got together, I thought I'd won the jackpot. Old family, money and contacts. I was green. Foolish. We married quickly once she got pregnant. But we were too young, and different. I wasn't much fun, with study and long hours. She wanted to party and be the life of the ball. I couldn't give that to her and by the time I left, I realised I'd made a mistake with her. But you were never a mistake, Davina."

"Throughout school, with every one of her new husbands or boyfriends, I hoped one would be my Daddy. They weren't." She gazed at him. "I see you with Carrie, Austin and even Josh, and I wish I'd had that. I'm not sure there's enough between us for that kind of relationship, to be honest, but I'd like to know you. To see what kind of relationship we can have as adults."

It was his turn to sigh and frown, and Davina understood her words had hurt him. It wasn't exactly what she wanted to do, but honesty had to be part of relationship they could forge.

"I failed you, Davina. Every day I didn't try harder. But I want you in my—in our life. Laura and I have a good marriage. We love our children and she's taught me you can make mistakes and learn from them."

Laura patted his hand. "The past is that. I can't change it, but Ashton and I have been talking since we had lunch at Bayside. Davina, would you be this baby's godmother? She's going to need someone smart and clever."

"A girl?" Now Davina beamed. Another half-sister. "I... I don't know how to be one, but if you really want me to, I'd be honoured."

Ashton rose. "I have something for you Davina." He disappeared inside and when he returned, it was with a small, framed photo. "This was taken about two weeks before your mother and I split up. I framed it and kept it with me."

"Oh!" Tears dribbled down her cheeks, scalding her. "You kept it?"

"He had it on his bedside table, the entire time I've known him, Davina."

She looked into her father's eyes and smiled. "Keep it, but I'd love a copy. Please." She meant it, because here was tangible proof that he'd loved her. Never really left her in his heart. "I don't have any photos of you. I think mother got rid of them when you left. Not even a wedding photo."

Ashton nodded. "Yes. It's the sort of thing she'd do."

Micah handed her a handkerchief, and she wiped her eyes. "We should go, but—"

"Don't be a stranger anymore, Davina. We're family."

&a,

"You enjoyed today, didn't you?" Micah watched as she stretched out, wriggling her feet.

"I did. I guess knowing that he didn't abandon me, and the opportunity to get to know my family isn't as bad as I thought."

He sipped at his wine. "Fenella wants to try something different next week. She's thinking maybe a barbeque rather than a meal. I like the idea. What do you think? The entire family is being asked what they think."

Her eyes glinted in the night. "Why are you asking me then?"

He grinned. "Because you're family now. Besides, you get to organize the next one." She tossed a pillow in his direction, he caught it and put it down. "So, what would you do for a family lunch?"

Davina scrunched up her nose, a thoroughly delightful display that captivated his attention. "I don't know. There's plenty of stuff, like we could go to the Escapades, a hike or in winter try out the skating rink."

"The skating rink? You've not seen Miriam on a bike. No sense of balance." He mimicked his sister falling over and she laughed.

"You're terrible, Micah! Aren't you supposed to love your sister?"

"Oh, I do, but that doesn't mean I can't take advantage of the opportunity to tease her that she can't stay upright on a bike, let alone skating blades."

"I'll have to ask her about what you did. You know, stuff that was embarrassing. Maybe I could post it on social media." He responded by growling and capturing her in his arms.

"Just you try," and he tickled her. His fingers started at her armpits, but as she moved, he grazed the side of her breasts and suddenly everything changed as her breath caught on a long moan.

The glasses went flying, white wine splashing, but it didn't matter because the heat rose between them.

Mouths jammed together as a heated kiss exploded.

Now there was no time for gentleness, because the scorching passion between them licked at him.

Micah welcomed it. The slow easy pace they'd become used to gone in an instant, replaced with a hunger that exceeded his control. It burned away the urbanity as he tore at her clothes.

Davina's hands found the clasp of his belt and jerked savagely, as if nothing could keep her from his skin, and he welcomed that.

Naked, illuminated only by the moonlight that filtered in, he gazed at her. His mouth dry, and his erection straining. Wanting.

"Micah?"

She rose, a goddess before him.

He wanted her as he'd never wanted another woman and the reality that she was his filled his soul with peace.

She scooped up the blanket he'd rested over the back of the lounge and a seed of devilry appeared in her gaze. "Follow me."

Davina led the way, leading him through the house, to his studio. When he made to pull her over to the chaise, she shook her head. "No." The smile she gave him this time was smoky, and she tossed him the blanket. "Hold this." She reached for the locks on the heavy wooden doors that led to the outside.

With a turn, Davina winked and beckoned him to join her. The warm salty air caressed his skin, and he followed her onto the grass, hidden from view by the trees and shrubs dotting the fence line. In the distance, the sea rolled and crashed.

With a deft manoeuvre, Micah flicked the blanket, and she sank down, patted the surface. "Come here," his houri called.

"Meditate with me."

They assumed their favoured position, while his loins ached with unfulfilled need. He closed his eyes, concentrating on the universe until his body cooled and only the whoosh of the ocean and the night birds calling interrupted the silence. It felt like only a moment passed before the touch of her hand on him—her fingers splayed over his chest—surprised him. "Micah?"

He caught her hand, twining his fingers around hers. Holding her close.

Their gazes locked, and he breathed. The scent of the ocean and his woman invading his mind. Centred, he welcomed the passion that flowed this time, a river coursing through him from brain to feet and invading like a rivulet into every nerve of his being.

Now she pulled her hands away. "Let me." She slid her fingers—soft touches that barely glanced his flesh—over his shoulders as she rose.

Her breasts, nipples jutting proudly, caught his attention and puckered even tighter as his breath whispered over them. It never ceased to amaze him just how responsive she was. The way her body replied to him and his needs. His hungers.

Davina hissed as she moved forward. Then she slid down, impaling herself on his erection, legs winding around his waist in the Yab-Yum position.

She held still, her form hot and ripe.

The wet glove of her yoni gripping his lingam.

Micah moved slowly, easing his hips so she rode him, soft in the moonlight, her eyes glowing with the fever that found its mate in him.

Every undulation masked the growing need to fulfil her. Every nudge ratcheted his excitement to fever pitch. He ruthlessly contained it, instead sliding his hands around her back. Sliding over the miles of silky-smooth skin, muscles bunching and tightening beneath his fingers.

"I love to touch you, Davina," he whispered, and she shivered.

"The way you touch me makes me want you more. I feel wanted," she responded on a wispy tone.

His fingers found purchase on her waist, dug deep, and held her still, and he levered away just enough so the tips of her nipples grazed his chest.

In the moonlight, her eyes glittered. And he was sure he'd never forget this night. The promise it contained and the joy she gave him.

His need rose, crashed over him and this time, when he moved, it was purposeful, as he drove deep into her. "I'm going to love your forever."

She moaned, neck a column there for him to feast upon and he did, giving into the pleasure. Surrendering to it.

Every cry she gave, every shiver urging him to give her more.

They moved, the soft, almost shy gestures giving way to harsh, demanding actions.

She jerked in his arms, finding her release, and the milking sensation that encased his cock pushed Micah over the edge and he came. Hard.

They held tight to each other as their skin cooled.

"Wow," Davina muttered, and he agreed. This time she shivered, and Micah pushed away and reached for her.

"Come inside before you get cold."

When she rose, he lifted the blanket and slid it around her shoulders. Her fingers gripped his, and she smiled. "You should join me."

"I already did, remember?" Davina blushed a little.

Amazing, really, given the intimacies they'd shared recently that something so simple could embarrass her.

He led her inside, closed the door, and led her to the bedroom.

&.

Two Months Later

Davina entered the office and, with a lightness in her step, made her way to Melony's office. "Is he in?"

She'd purposefully dressed in casual attire.

Mel's surprise filled Davina with pleasure. She knew none of had been sure she'd go ahead with her plan, but the release it gave her, boosted her emotionally. Together with the knowledge she could balance her life, gave her the anchor she'd needed for so long.

Micah. He'd given her the life she would soon live. Not that he'd given it to her per se... No, he'd just helped her understand that what she wanted was achievable.

"I'll just check." Mel picked up the phone and tagged the man in the room beyond.

Jim opened the door and peered out. "Davina?"

"I just need a minute of your time, Jim." She advanced, and he opened the door. "Mel, you might like to come in too."

She knew neither of them yet knew for sure the reason for her odd request, though they'd likely wondered. She'd clutched it to herself for the last few days, having only told Micah that morning what she'd decided.

So, when she took up the seat opposite the heavy wood partner's desk, they looked at her. "I've been struggling for a while, Jim. You know I've taken time off in the last couple of months to see to personal tasks. I've decided I'm not returning to work and will retrain. My intention is to practice Conveyancing Law."

"We knew you were unhappy and guessed you were planning to leave," he said, "but conveyancing?"

Her light laugh filled the air. "It feels right. I can work with families at a high point in their lives. Be part of something positive that allows me to give back. To help without losing myself in the system. So, now that Jane's case is completed, I'm giving a month's notice, but I've got more leave and I'm taking it. As a result, I won't be back to work."

Their jaws dropped. "Not back?"

She shook her head. "No. I have no more cases, so I'm extending my leave, and it's not like I'm leaving anything incomplete. There's no need for me to apprise anyone else of files or cases. I'm sorry to leave like this, but I've enrolled in some courses at the university. The first refresher starts in two weeks, and I plan to attend that first. Then I'm planning to go it alone. A single operator."

She rose. "Thank you, Jim and Mel. Your guidance and help were invaluable, but it's time to do this for me."

She'd contact Mel in the next few days and arrange a coffee date, something she hadn't done in aeons.

Davina hitched up her purse, slung it over her shoulder and left. Micah waited in her office, boxes in hand, and she packed up the few personal possessions, her law books and photos.

They had left the building when her mobile phone rang and she answered, knowing instinctively who it was. "Hi Elyse. I haven't heard from you since your trip to Bali with Doctor Delicious. Are you around today?"

"Wow, that's a welcoming. You've been pretty absent yourself lately and yes, I've got time."

"Good, because I'm bringing someone with me, and I have lots to tell you. Bring your Doctor Delicious too," she laughed.

"Oh, I would, but he and I are kaput. He wanted a commitment. I didn't, so its bye-bye and time to find a new squeeze. But I'll meet you at that new restaurant. Have you been to Bayside yet?"

Davina laughed. "Oh yes. See you at midday then."

Micah caught her gaze. "Doctor Delicious?"

"Wait until you meet Elyse and that will explain a lot." They left the building and loaded the boxes into her car, and she climbed into the driver's seat. "We're having lunch at Bayside with my best friend, Elyse. She's the one who encouraged me to go to Knights Meditation Haven, so it's all her fault," she chuckled.

Micah barked a laugh as they headed north to the beachside and they found a park some distance from the restaurant. Hand in hand they wandered the shops on the road until it was time to meet her friend and once inside she watched as Elyse scanned the crowd, her gaze startled when it settled on Micah.

"Well, well. So, meditation has its benefits then?" her friend crowed, and Davina laughed.

"I've told him everything, including that you're my best friend."

CHAPTER
TWENTY-ONE

Three Months Later

Micah's hand clenched on the steering wheel in the half light as they drove down the road to the meeting point. The small bus the company provided idled, and he pulled into the parking lot.

Davina climbed out, and with a grin flashed at him, sauntered to the bus. He followed, watching the sway of her hips, which eased his fears for a few moments. Once their names were checked off the list, they climbed aboard, and Micah took her hand.

"This is going to be fantastic," she enthused while his stomach knotted.

A few others climbed aboard, and the bus inched forward, heading for the location of the balloon launch site.

Three enormous air balloons waited, the hiss of heated air inflating them echoing in the silence. Everyone who'd boarded the bus looked at the balloons. He and Davina—thankfully just the two of them — moved to the bright pink one, emblazoned with a dove.

"Help me in," she asked, and he lifted her, hands on her hips as she kicked her feet forward, landing in the large basket. He followed her over the side and the pilot ran them through the drills they needed to know.

Workers scurried around and soon it was time for them to rise into the sky, as long fingers of orange and red erupted over the horizon.

"Look," called Davina and pointed to his house in the distance. "There's the house!"

He wound his arm around her, and they held on as the balloon floated over the bay. Day started dawning, and the air warmed slightly, though the cool weather of late autumn meant they needed heavy coats.

Her gaze turned to him, shone and not for the first time, he thanked providence for bringing this woman into his life.

They looked over the side and she pointed out places they knew and all the while; he watched the play of excitement on her face, wondering if this was the right decision. *No turning back now.*

The balloon started its descent, slow and cautious, to the large cordoned off park. His car at the end along with those of his family.

Once on the ground, they were met with glasses of champagne and he towed her over to where his family waited, beyond the barrier.

"That was fantastic," she enthused to Miriam, who hugged her.

Fenella and the kids had already laid out the mat, his brother Simeon carrying the hamper over from the car.

Micah looked to Noah, and his brother nodded, letting Micah know he'd brought the item he'd requested Noah deliver. In the distance, he noted Ashton pulling up, Laura beside him and their three children. They'd join them for the picnic, Laura having insisted on bringing her own contribution.

They sank to one of the mats which Fenella and Miriam had

brought. He tugged Davina close, wallowing in the serenity that came from her presence and the way she now interacted comfortably with his family. When Ashton, Laura, Carrie, Austin, and tiny baby Jennifer joined them, the noise of happy families welled.

As a family, they pulled out the meats, fruits and salads, the drinks, plates, and cups. Everyone dug in while Miriam prattled away. "I've never been in a hot-air balloon. Was it cold?"

Davina giggled, "Cool, but I think in say summer it would be lovely enough to just wear a light top. Fenella this salad is delicious. I think you should give Micah the recipe so he can make it for me!"

Fenella quizzed her about when she'd open her firm to offer conveyancing services and she chattered away about office space, assistants, and advertising.

As far as Davina knew, today was to celebrate her completion of the refresher courses she'd taken to change fields.

The adults who knew what was happening passed the time, watching the children play chase on the grass, now that the cordon was lifted, with the balloons stored away for another week and chatting about life. Laura fed baby Jennifer under the shade of the tree while Davina and her father spoke about his family. She'd been spending time with him, learning the history of the family she never knew.

Micah was handed baby Jennifer by a knowing Ashton. Then her father passed Davina another glass of champagne. Ashton whispered to Micah, "When?"

As Micah answered with "soon." Jennifer fretted, and Micah handed the baby back to Laura. He knew he'd need to capture Davina's attention soon as the clock tower in the centre of the park bonged out the hour of one.

The anticipation inside him climbed to fever pitch, and he sweated, hoping she'd think it was purely because they were outside under the sun.

Fenella packed up her hamper and slid it to one side, Miriam and Davina assisting, then they ushered the children to the bathroom.

"You've got the box, Noah?"

Noah passed it over, and he took the velvet case, opened it. There lay the item he'd asked for from the family. Now he slipped it inside his pocket, having wanted to not have any chance of Davina even having a clue. He'd also not wanted to lose it in case it fell out of his pocket while in the balloon. The symbolism of it far too important.

The women and children returned, and the roar of an engine overhead had him turning. He looked up and smiled. "Hey Davina, look up."

As a group, everyone on the mat gazed up, except him. He turned his attention fully to Davina. Waiting with his heart in his hands for her response.

The plane flying over soared, trailing the banner. *Marry me, Davina.*

When she squeaked and turned, he had the small box in his hands open. His mother's ring glinted in the sun.

"Marry me, Davina. Make me the happiest man in the world."

Tears glinted as she smiled and nodded. "I will!"

The family laughed and clapped their pleasure at her answer as he reached down, took the ring from the case, and slipped it on her finger.

"I will always be your family and you will always be the first person on my mind in the morning and the last at night. I will stand by you when times are hard and enjoy your successes. Because I love you, Davina."

"It's beautiful, Micah. How did you pick it, though?"

Noah cleared his throat. "It was Mum's. She left it to Micah, but we all agreed, you should wear it because you've made Micah so happy, and above all, Mum would have loved you for that."

She caught a sob behind her hand. For a moment, he wondered if he'd made the wrong choice. *Should I have bought her a new one?*

"It's the most beautiful ring ever. I'll be forever proud to wear if Simeon, Miriam, and Noah don't mind? Most of all because she left it to you Micah for this reason and you gave it to me."

She reached over now, flung her arms around him, and kissed him as tears streamed down her cheeks.

The family cheered them on, and he pulled away with a laugh.

"Did you get all of that, Laura?"

Davina's stepmother laughed and held up the camera. "Everything."

As the sun beat down, two large families came together to celebrate the beginning of another, because once more, love overcame darkness.

If you enjoyed this book by Imogene Nix why not check out some more of her titles by checking out the following pages?

INHERITANCE OF THE BLOOD BY IMOGENE NIX

In the darkness evil waits...

As a young bride Kira was whisked away from everything and everyone she knew, including her new husband and became Christina, an operative of the Displaced Persons Unit.

As the danger grows she sees an opportunity to save her husband

Vasya and sister Serina. But nothing is the same. Serina is grown up —married and pregnant.

Vasya too is older and darkly forbidding. Trusting Christina doesn't come easily until a catastrophic event takes place. Now, knowing the truth everything he thought he knew is changed. But at a very high cost.

The four must work together to defeat the Demon, Zuor and the stakes are higher than they imagined and all could be lost.

———————————

The burning at the back of her neck warned she was being watched. A quick glance didn't clarify it. Instead, she turned around in time to see her mother's face, pale. "Mama?"

She took a step forward, but her grandfather snatched her wrist.

The grip was painful, and Kira stilled. "Let your parents talk."

She didn't know what the topic of conversation was, but it couldn't be good.

The dappled sunlight seemed cooler than before.

Her father crooked his forefinger at her grandfather while they stood there. For a moment she wished Vasya had come with them, but he had to work. Just the thought of her new husband warmed Kira.

She only had a few minutes to contemplate her newly defined status as a married woman, when her grandfather pulled at her hand. "Come with me." He tugged and, confused, Kira allowed herself to be towed away.

A glance at her parents' faces stole any feeling of well-being.

"Grandfather?"

"Shh, my love. You must go." His grip was implacable and his face stern, but he shivered.

"What are you doing? Where are you taking me, Grandfather?"

They moved rapidly through the village they'd visited to sell their wares just that morning, and for the first time since they'd arrived in the market place she felt fear. What was wrong? Was it something to do with Vasya?

"You are in danger. We must send you away." The words confused her further. Send her away? Danger?

"Where is Vasya?" She stumbled over a stone, but he kept tugging her onwards.

With a quick glance around, he hauled her into a dirty laneway between the buildings. Kira gasped, trying to drag air into her starving lungs. "There's no time. We must get you away."

A nondescript shopfront lay ahead, and he pushed on the door. It rattled and opened with a loud groan. "Andre? Andre, are you here?"

An older man shuffled into the room, bent nearly double from the weight of the load on his back. "Marat? What do you want?"

"My granddaughter. They are coming for her and us. Get her away. Take her now, while you can."

The man's face clouded over. "Are you sure?"

"Grandfather, where is Vasya?" Fright had the blood in her veins pounding.

"Hush, my precious. Andre will see you well." He turned. "Whatever it takes, Andre. Take her now." With surprising speed, her grandfather whirled and was gone.

The man, Andre, eyed her. "Come this way, child. There is no time to be lost."

Eleven years later

The tattoo of her heart and cry of terror woke her, as they usually did. Once again, as she had since that rapid flight from those who sought her, she found herself in a lonely bed. Hundreds of miles away from everything she'd dreamed of, in a house she'd built for them to share. As always, it left her wishing that Vasya had fled with her.

Instead, here she was, exiled without her husband. With a sob, she rolled over and let the tears fall.

Available from Beachwalk Press

books2read.com/IOTB

THE CELTIC CUPID TRILOGY

When Cupid—otherwise known as Diocail— is banished from his home on a remote Scottish Island, he's set a series of tasks by the great god Lugh, who also happens to be his father.

In **Blame The Wine,** he must bring two lovers together... BBW Cara and James, the man she's lusted over from afar who happens to be a super geek and head Veha Industries.

In **A Stranger's Embrace,** Diocail is driven to help an emotionally fragile Jane and Davis, a famous author. The task is more complicated, with the existence of Carstairs her could-be ex-husband and teenage daughter, Frannie.

In **Revenge on Cupid**, Diocail must take the ultimate chance and find his own happily ever after with Simone. Sometimes the past gets in the way and HEA's don't come cheap though.

The dusty, dingy little diner was full, even with its current state of cleanliness—or lack thereof. People from the surrounding offices didn't care about anything except the incredible, well-prepared food at a reasonable cost. They flooded in, like waves to the shore. As one tide left, another swept in.

"Honestly, Simone. I'm going to try getting his attention one more time. If that doesn't work, I'm out of there. I mean, how long can I keep trying?" Cara picked at the caramel tart she hadn't been able to resist with the cheap metal fork and flicked the blob of fresh cream that sat on top to the side of the plate.

"You've said that tons of times before. Besides, what are you going to do to get his attention? Hmm? Walk naked through the typing pool?" Simone bobbed the straw in her smoothie as she eyed her friend with a frown. "It's been what? Eighteen months since you saw him, and you've mooned over him from a distance ever since you met him. You need to move on, Cara. That is, unless there's something you haven't shared?"

The query was arch. Cara shivered even as she shook her head. "No."

Simone quirked an eyebrow, obviously unconvinced with the answer. Cara let out a deep sigh of frustration. "There's a position…it's only temporary, for a PA reporting directly to him." She speared a forkful of tart, chewed quickly and swallowed, before continuing. "In his office, full-time for the period of the engagement. I saw the memo yesterday. I mean, I have the skills, right? I can type, answer phones, make coffee, file, greet people. What's more, I can probably do it better than all those size eights in the typing pool that

Ms. Jackman seems to prefer." She nodded thoughtfully. "All I have to do is get past the ogre in Human Resources."

Simone stared at her, disbelief clear on her face. "Girl, I so remember that woman. If you think you can get past her, you're doing better than I ever did. That's why I left Veha Industries, remember? Maybe it's time to haul out your resumé and consider some other options. Look for something better." Simone shook her head and billows of her crimson hair swirled through the still air.

Cara understood Simone only had her best interests at heart. But this time she knew the outcome would be different. Hell, she could feel it in the air. The tingle of expectation.

"Cara, the HR ogre will hang you out for breakfast before she offers you anything like a position in that office. Remember her mantra? Good looks and good work make for a positive workplace!"

Simone didn't sugar-coat anything. It was another great reason for their long- term friendship. Honesty. But Cara didn't want to hear the truth in the statement. Even if it was exactly as her friend said.

Cara nodded quickly. "Yeah, I know, but if I don't try, then I won't know how close I can get to him, right? And the only way to catch his attention is to get past *her* and see him in person." Cara quaked a little at the information she needed to share. The favor she needed to ask. "Anyway, I tidied up my resumé and dropped the application into a memo envelope yesterday, so it's too late to back out now. I mean, fortune favors the brave. Doesn't it? If I don't snag an interview, I'm going to visit the career advisor across the street and register with them." She shrugged. "I'll look for temp work until something more long-term shows up. I can see what they have on offer and well...who knows? Maybe a job with the right boss is just waiting for me. But I'd rather this worked out, to be honest." Her voice trailed off into a whisper. "I really wish he would notice me."

Simone took a long slurp of her banana drink, and Cara noticed her questioning gaze even as she squirmed. Finally, Simone nodded. "It's your funeral. So anyway, you'd better show me this memo if you want me to be a referee for you. I'm guessing that's what you need, right? I'll have to know what I'm supposed to say about you before they ring."

Cara smiled. "Thanks, Simone. I knew I could count on you." She slipped a piece of paper out of her handbag and handed it over. "Sorry it's a bit creased. It was in the bottom of my bag, I stashed it so none of the others from the pool would see. You know how it is."

Available from Love Books Publishing
books2read.com/CelticCupid

Direct Autographed Copy
http://bit.ly/2vs7wtS

BIOCYBE BY IMOGENE NIX

Can a cyber-enhanced warrior and a ship's captain find love together?

Levia Endrado never wanted to be a warrior, but at seventeen she was deemed suitable for battle. After intense training and multiple enhancements, which gave her superior strength and healing ability, she was sent off to defeat the enemy—a killing machine with a mission.

When the war was over, she had to find a new life. At twenty-seven she's a washed-up veteran without a future. Or she was, until she met Sandon Daria.

Serving as a pilot aboard Sandon's spaceship the *Golden Echo* makes Levia long for a different and gentler life. But old hurts and even older enemies aren't so easily forgotten. Particularly when they come back for her.

Sandon is determined to show Levia that she's more than just a BioCybe...she's the woman who completes him. Getting close is just the first step, keeping her alive is an even bigger challenge, but one he's willing to take because the prize is their combined future.

––––––––––––––––

Levia scanned the long line of other hopefuls entering the chamber. The large building in the center of town was cold, and she dragged her wrap around her body, even as she craned her head, looking to the high ceiling. She'd never before had an occasion to enter the testing complex, yet she'd seen the lines of teenagers every time they passed the building.

Once she'd asked her parents why the teens were lined up and her mother's face had shuttered. Her stepfather had just shaken his head and growled. They'd stopped her questions with a carefully uttered, "You'll know soon enough, Levia." The pain in her mother's eyes had been enough to shush her questions. For endless months afterward, her parents had traveled different routes to the educational facility she attended and Levia lost interest in the puzzle of that building.

Now, as she looked around, remembering that long ago spring day, it was her opportunity to find out. But she felt a surge of concern at what lay ahead. She likely wasn't the only one, given that there were probably two to three hundred seventeen-year-olds gathered in the one place. Ahead of her, she caught sight of a couple of girls, their arms linked together and wide smiles on their faces. Scanning the crowd, she became aware that, by far, a majority of those gathered displayed both fear and trepidation.

"All female subjects will enter through doors three, six, and seven. All male subjects will enter through gates four, eight, and ten." The speaker above her was loud, and she jumped before checking the numbers etched on the black metal sign over her head.

The massive doors beside her swung open, and now an uncertain silence reigned. Many of the youngsters hung back, clearly discomforted by whatever testing regime lay ahead. This was where they'd been told their futures would be determined.

"Oh gosh, I hope they only have an aptitude and psych eval. I don't think..." Levia turned to see the white face of the girl behind her. The girl had uttered what many must silently be thinking.

Levia dragged an unsteady breath in, her hand resting flat against the plane of her belly as she looked around. No one had entered yet. It was clear many were on the verge of taking the step, but still they hung back.

She straightened her shoulders. "I'm not afraid." It was always wiser to approach things head-on, she believed. When her biological father had died, she'd been one of the few to view his capsule before it was sent into the massive gray structure built to accommodate those who'd moved onto the next life realm.

Her legs shook as she wobbled toward the entrance. Beyond the doorway, she spied sealed cubicles and her heart stuttered. Why cubicles? Usually testing—med and psych—were in eval-units, hidden only by billowing white curtains. She glanced back, noting that others had taken the first step.

"Move along, subjects." Once again, the androgynous voice of the address system blared.

Of course, given it was her seventeenth anniversary of birth, she was technically considered an adult now.

She thought longingly of baby Rald and her half-sister, Elda, waiting at home for her to return, and the celebrations to be held that night. That made her smile. She would need to make them proud of her.

She entered a row and the tall Educational Specialist, the edu-specs as her peers laughingly called them, stopped her. "Present your credentials to the scanner."

She'd done this many times since the tiny implant had been slipped below the dermal layer of her skin at birth. The small unit in her wrist heated as her details were checked.

"Enter the first cubicle, Levia Endrado, and follow the instructions to complete your assessment."

Thus dismissed, Levia moved to the first unit, laid her palm against the scanner, and the door slid open soundlessly.

"Welcome, Levia Endrado. Take your place in the eval-unit." The soft contralto of the voice echoed after the door closed silently behind her.

"What are you evaluating?" Her voice was breathy, and she peered around.

"Your skills—physical and psychological. Your emotional and medical status. Your educational attainment levels."

It was an answer that shed little insight into the many things she was hungry to know. "Why do all seventeen year olds—"

"Take a seat, Levia. Then we may begin your testing."

If she'd expected an answer, she was sadly mistaken, she considered sourly. She dropped into the seat, the soft leather-like surface molding to her body.

"Levia Endrado, you are required to remove all non-specified apparel."

She jolted in the chair. "It's cold."

"The temperature will be amended. Remove the non-specified apparel."

Her misgivings grew as she dragged off the light wrap she'd brought with her, and then threw it to the floor at the side of the unit.

"We will begin, Levia Endrado. At any time, should you experience any malfunctions of the unit, simply depress the red button." It glowed and she grimaced.

Levia reclined against the chair and waited for the testing to begin.

The first examination was based on her understanding of the political system, where she saw herself, and her knowledge of the rights and responsibilities accorded through citizenship of both her planet and the commonwealth.

The second test was mathematical and scientific proficiency. It felt like hours had passed by the time she'd finished, and she lay limp on the seat, exhausted.

"Levia Endrado, you may rise. The sanitary unit will emerge once you trigger the yellow button at the door. Should you require refreshment, press the blue button and a restorative will be made available."

"Can I leave?"

"Negative, Levia Endrado. Your needs will be catered for in this capsule."

"Why?" Her voice hitched and true fear rose for the first time. Why did they keep her in the alcove?

"All will be revealed at the end of the testing cycle."

Levia looked at the now empty screen before hurling a curse word. It was met with silence.

The urgent throb of her bladder reminded her that she needed to use the facilities, so, with

a sigh, she rose and clambered from the seat. After attending to the needs of her body, she walked around the unit, peering at the door, but it was obviously programmed remotely. She poked and prodded, but it made no difference. With a huff, she headed back to the chair.

The moment she'd settled in, the viewing screen shone bright. "Welcome back, Levia. The next sequence will evaluate your psychological reflexes, then that will be followed up with the general knowledge portion of the evaluation."

"When can I leave?" It seemed better to ask bluntly, she told herself.

"Once the examination is completed. After the next set of evaluations, you will be subjected to the physical aspect."

"Then I can go home?"

"Levia Endrado, you will now complete the psychological test. This will be undertaken by one of the center's personal evaluators."

She frowned. Personal evaluators? She bit her lip, and the sting reminded her that this wasn't something to joke about. In her seventeen years, she'd only heard of personal evaluators being brought in once before, and that was when one of the girls at her academy had been in a serious accident. Both legs were amputated and her body's ability to keep her alive had been gravely compromised. Her peers had been informed that the girl had requested the assessment before she could request her support systems be disconnected.

"Levia Endrado, are you ready to recommence processing?" The emotionless voice echoed once more and she gulped.

"Yes."

Available from Beachwalk Press
http://www.beachwalkpress.com

Direct Autographed Books
http://bit.ly/BioCybe

Also by Imogene Nix

Warriors of the Elector

- Star of Ishtar
- Starline
- Starfire
- Star of the Fleet
- Starburst
- The Star of Eternity

The Star of Ishtar & Starline - Print

Starfire & Star of the Fleet - Print

Starburst & The Star of Eternity - Print

The Secrets World:

Blood Secrets

- The Blood Bride
- The Illuminated Witch
- The Sorcerer's Touch

House Secrets

- As Dawn Breaks
- Immortal Consequences
- Unnamed Book III

All That Glitters - a House Secrets Novella (Coming in 2023)

Danu's Secrets

- The Downfall of Padraic O'Shaunessy (Coming in 2023)
- Unnamed Secrets Book II

The Automaton Series

- Haven House (Coming April 2022)
- Nobel Crest (Coming July 2022)

The Search Duology

- Miss Elspeth's Desire
- Miss Isabelle's Craving

Reunion Trilogy

- War's End
- The Assassin
- Executing Justice

The Reunion Trilogy in Paperback

Sex Love & Aliens

- Tangled Webs
- False Webs
- Covert Webs

21st Testing Protocol

- Cyborg: Redux
- Children Of A Greater Evil
- When Evil Came To Stay
- Finis: The War To End All Wars

Celtic Cupid Trilogy

- Blame The Wine
- A Stranger's Embrace
- Revenge On Cupid

The Celtic Cupid Trilogy in Paperback

Zombieology

- The Reset (re-releasing Feb 2022)
- I Dream of Zombies
- The Six Million Dollar Zombie
- Make Room For Zombies
- Unnamed Zombiology Book (coming 2023)

Knights of Pleasure - A Tantric Exploration Series

- Silken Knights (Coming in September 2022)

Single Titles

The Chocolate Affair (also in Print)

Falling In Love Again (Previously A Sapphire For Karina)

BioCybe (also in Print)

Hesparia's Tears (also in Print)

Tomorrow's Promise

A Bar In Paris (also in Print)

Inheritance Of The Blood (also in Print)

The Plan

Loving Memories (also in Print)

Hero of Heartbreak Hill (also in Print)

My One & Only

Curse Bound (coming 2021)

Raspberry Dreams (Not Yet Released)

Non Fiction

Self Publishing: Absolute Beginners Guide (With Suzi Love)

Written as Ciara Cave

25 Curated Ways To Get Rid Of Telemarketers

Book Signings for Absolute Beginners

About the Author

Imogene is published in a range of romance genres including Paranormal, Science Fiction and Contemporary. She is mainly published in the UK and USA.

In 2010, Imogene Nix (the pen name not Imogene herself) was born. Imogene sat down and worked tirelessly for 3 months culminating in the book Starline, which became the first in a trilogy titled, "Warriors of the Elector." Since then she's had over 30 titles published and is now focusing on hybridising herself - with a mixture of traditionally published and self-published works.

In fact, she's taking control of many of her back catalogue books, which are slowly re-releasing as self-published titles.

Imogene is a member of a range of professional organisations world wide, and believes in the mantra of mentoring and paying it forward and is actively involved in mentorship (through NaNoWrimo and her vlog: In The Chair With Imogene Nix) and tutoring of new and upcoming authors.

In her spare time she loves to drink coffee, wine & eat chocolate and is parenting her spoiled dog and a ferocious cat along with her husband and 2 human daughters and looks forward to weekends away with her husband in their caravan "The Seven Year Hitch!" Do look forward to her caravan romance at some point!

To Contact Imogene
www.imogenenix.net
imogene@imogenenix.net

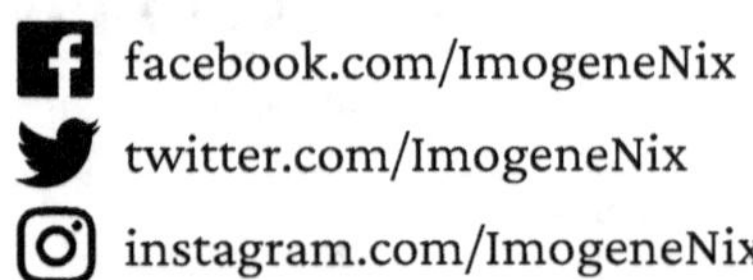

facebook.com/ImogeneNix
twitter.com/ImogeneNix
instagram.com/ImogeneNix

www.ingramcontent.com/pod-product-compliance
Lightning Source LLC
Chambersburg PA
CBHW071157180726
48291CB00007B/2496